"I now declare you husband and wife."

It took a moment for the words to sink in.

"You may kiss your bride."

Karina's gaze flew to Luke's. He was a stranger. And her new husband. For the first time she saw something else flickering in his steady gaze. Something that sent a jolt through her system and suddenly made her very nervous.

She somehow wasn't prepared for the instant when his lips met hers. The first caress was brief, experimental. The second immediately deepened the kiss, his lips firm and strong and sure.

Behind their closed lids, her eyes rolled back as she let the wave of sensations carry her away, pushing aside everything she'd lived with for the past few months.

Then it was over.

She tried to calm her suddenly racing heart and understand exactly why a pretend kiss had felt so amazingly real.

KERRY CONNOR

TRUSTING *a* STRANGER

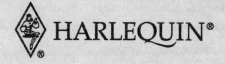

HARLEQUIN®

TORONTO • NEW YORK • LONDON
AMSTERDAM • PARIS • SYDNEY • HAMBURG
STOCKHOLM • ATHENS • TOKYO • MILAN • MADRID
PRAGUE • WARSAW • BUDAPEST • AUCKLAND

To Vanessa, for twenty-five years of friendship, and for being the kind of friend who was almost happier than I was when I finally sold a book to Harlequin Intrigue.

Recycling programs
for this product may
not exist in your area.

ISBN-13: 978-0-373-69437-2

TRUSTING A STRANGER

Copyright © 2009 by Kerry Connor

ABOUT THE AUTHOR

A lifelong mystery reader, Kerry Connor first discovered romantic suspense by reading Harlequin Intrigue books and is thrilled to be writing for the line. Kerry lives and writes in Southern California.

Books by Kerry Connor

HARLEQUIN INTRIGUE
1067—STRANGERS IN THE NIGHT
1094—BEAUTIFUL STRANGER
1129—A STRANGER'S BABY
1170—TRUSTING A STRANGER

CAST OF CHARACTERS

Karina Fedorova—Caught in an impossible situation, her only hope of survival is to marry a stranger.

Luke Hubbard—He has no interest in letting anyone into his life, but he can't refuse to help Karina. Even if the only way to protect her is to marry her.

Dmitri Fedorov—Karina's first husband crossed the wrong man, and left her to deal with the consequences.

Anton Solokov—He will stop at nothing to obtain the information he believes Karina possesses, and exact the punishment he thinks she deserves.

Sergei Yevchenko—He paid the ultimate price for trying to protect Karina.

Viktor Yevchenko—Luke's old friend picked up the mission to protect Karina after his father's death. Would he suffer the same fate?

Prologue

A sharp gust of wind grabbed the branches of the trees outside the window, sending them crashing and scratching against the glass with a screech.

From where she stood in front of the window, the impact came mere inches from Karina's face. She didn't even flinch. She had too many actual threats to fear to be so easily frightened by nothing.

As she had every day since her arrival, she stared out at the street in front of the building. She watched the passing cars, she scanned the pedestrians. She didn't know why she kept her silent vigil. There was really nothing to see. If the danger she expected did come, it would hardly approach so boldly from the front. The answers she sought deep in her soul weren't out there. Yet she simply didn't know what else to do.

She'd arrived in the United States just over a month ago at the beginning of February. From what she'd seen through the building's windows, it had been gray and cold ever since. Not so unlike Russia at this time of year.

She almost wished she could look at the unremarkable city scene outside and pretend she was home. But she'd never managed to forget that she was not home, nor why.

"I am going out now."

The booming voice behind her was too familiar to startle her. Or perhaps she was simply too numb to be startled.

Forcing some semblance of a smile, Karina turned to face her godfather. He stood halfway inside the room, already wearing his overcoat, pulling on his gloves. He was a big, robust man with a ruddy face automatically eased in a smile of his own. But she sensed the strain in his expression as much as she felt it in her own. He couldn't quite hide the worry in his eyes. Even though he'd said nothing about it, she knew how much trouble he'd gone to to bring her here. She hated that she'd brought her problems halfway around the world to his door, but she'd simply had nowhere else to go.

"You should come with me," Sergei said. "Come see the city. You have not left this building since you arrived."

"I am fine here." *Safe here.*

"You are not fine," he said, the reprimand slightly tempered. "You are hiding."

"For good reason."

He grimaced. "I brought you here to be safe, not to turn this building into your prison."

"It is too nice to be a prison," Karina said wearily. She cast an eye around the room. Beautifully decorated, it was as lovely as the rest of Sergei's home. Much like the homes she used to decorate back in Moscow, when she'd had a job, a life that was not limited to four walls. How unfortunate that the plush surroundings were wasted on her.

She felt him watching her. "There are many kinds of prisons," he said. "You know, the Americans like to say this is the land of the free." He smiled, a trace of patronizing amusement in his voice.

Her lips quirked sadly. "But it is not my land. Perhaps I am right not to feel free here."

"You are safe here," he said, echoing her earlier thoughts. But hearing the words spoken aloud merely allowed a whisper of doubt to creep in.

Still she answered, "I know." But she couldn't meet his eyes.

Sergei stepped forward and took her hands. "We will not let him win."

Dread pooled in her belly. He could say the words a thousand times and she didn't think she would be able to believe them.

Lowering her head so he couldn't see the doubt on her face, she could only nod tightly.

He pressed a kiss to her forehead and stepped away.

Karina listened to the sound of his retreating footsteps, the soft click of the door shutting, letting the warmth of his words and his touch sink in as she tried to believe he was right. They failed to pierce the bone-deep cold filling her body.

She wrapped her arms around herself, even though the chill had nothing to do with the temperature, and slowly regained her position at the window. The wind had picked up again. The branches in the trees twisted and tangled like the frenzied writhing of tormented spirits.

Or the ever-present uneasiness she felt churning deep within her that not even Sergei's assurances could calm.

KARINA HAD LONG SINCE retreated to the sofa, night having fallen hours earlier, when she heard the voices. The sound of them, their tone sharp and urgent, broke into her thoughts. She frowned, irritated by the distraction even if nothing she'd been thinking about had been particularly pleasant.

She slowly raised her head to look at the closed door, the one Sergei had shut when he left. The barrier was thick, solid. Yet the voices were loud enough, the intensity in them fierce enough, to be heard through the surface.

A familiar sense of foreboding fell over her. She tried to swallow, only to discover her mouth had suddenly gone dry.

Something was wrong.

Part of her longed to stay where she was, safely insulated from whatever lay on the other side of that door.

The rest of her already knew what it was, what it had to be. What she'd feared would happen from the moment Sergei had brought her here, even more than the idea of something happening to her.

She barely realized she was rising from her seat until her feet hit the floor. As if in a trance, she forced herself to cross the room and open the door.

One of the household staff stood a short distance down the hallway. At the sight of her, Karina's heart fell into her stomach. The woman's hand was pressed to her mouth, her expression locked in grief and horror and shock.

And Karina knew she'd been right.

"What's wrong?" she asked, the voice seeming to come from far away rather than from her own mouth.

The woman jerked her head up and just stared at her for a long moment. It didn't seem possible, but the horror on her face deepened at the sight of Karina standing there.

"Mr. Yevchenko— He…is dead."

Expecting it did nothing to protect her from the sharp pain that ripped through her at hearing the words spoken. She realized some small part had hoped that it would not be true, or that if something had to have happened, he would only be hurt, not killed.

"How?" she asked, that strange, distant voice coming out as a barely audible rasp.

"A shooting. He was leaving his vehicle and a car drove by. Someone inside shot at him."

Of course, she thought faintly. That was how they would do it. She didn't ask if the shooter had been caught. She knew better than to think they would choose a way that would lead to them being captured.

She stood frozen, unable to move, unable to react, unable to do anything but stare at the horror on the woman's face, knowing it was mirrored on her own.

The woman started to say something else. Karina didn't hear her, the sound drowned out by Sergei's final words to her, the reassurances now painfully mocking, echoing in her ears.

You are safe here.
We will not let him win.

And another voice, one she usually only heard in her nightmares, now as vivid as though the speaker were standing beside her, whispering cruelly in her ear.

I always win.

Chapter One

Karina stared at the closed door in front of her and did her best to calm her racing heart. "I don't know if I can do this."

She felt the man beside her look down at her. "Do you have any other ideas?" Viktor asked.

"No." If she had she would have said so before now. Heaven knew she had spent enough time thinking about it in the past week. How Sergei's death was her fault, and how would she survive.

It was Viktor, Sergei's son, who had come up with this option, this man. The one person who might be able to help her.

Her entire life. Her hope of survival. All in the hands of a stranger.

Trying not to shift nervously from one foot to the other like a child, she glanced up at Viktor. "Do you think he will even agree to this?"

"I do not know," he said simply. "But it is a chance."

Yes, it is, she agreed silently. One so extreme she wasn't sure she could go through with it, even if the man did agree.

But first he needed to answer the door and let them in. She sent an uneasy glance behind her, feeling entirely too exposed standing on the front stoop of this house. Even as she did, she sensed Viktor doing the same. It was impossible not to remember what had happened to Sergei and feel just how vulnerable they were out in the open.

The door finally opened in response to Viktor's earlier knock.

Viktor had told her several things about the man they'd driven to Baltimore from Washington, D.C., to see. What he looked like had not been one of them. She hadn't asked, the subject seeming unimportant compared to everything else. So she could only stare blankly at the man who'd answered the door, his expression solemn, and wait for either man's reaction.

"Viktor," the man at the door said finally, his mouth curving slightly at one corner. "It's been a while."

"Too long," Viktor agreed with a shadow of the charming smile she'd seen him wield since childhood.

As the two men shook hands, Karina carefully studied the man who'd answered the door. So this must be Luke Hubbard, Viktor's old friend. Her best chance.

She'd tried to picture what he might look like, but nothing she'd imagined had come close to the man himself. He was a big man, tall and broad-shouldered, dressed casually in a white polo shirt and dark slacks. His was a handsome face, but there was a hardness to it, with so many sharp angles and hard planes, that gave him more of an edge than she'd expected. He most likely was the same age as Viktor, which would make him thirty-three.

Viktor said he was an attorney. Corporate law or something to do with business. Yes, she could imagine this man being a formidable opponent in a business negotiation. Perhaps he would be for Solokov, as well.

He would need to be.

"I was sorry to hear about your father," Luke Hubbard said.

"Thank you." Viktor nodded shortly, his expression tensing with grief.

It had been only a week, and Karina knew only too well that the pain of his father's death remained fresh. She felt the sorrow of it, too, combined with a guilt that was hers alone.

Her godfather was dead for one reason only: because he'd tried to help her.

And now she'd come to ask this man for his help. To put himself in danger for her. Guilt stabbed at her again. It didn't seem right to involve, to risk, anyone else. But then, what choice did she have?

"And thank you for agreeing to see us," Viktor was saying. At the obvious cue, he reached over and prodded her forward slightly with the press of his hand against the small of her back. "Allow me to introduce Karina Andreevna Fedorova. Our families have long been good friends. My father was her godfather."

She forced a smile onto her face as the man finally turned his attention to her.

The smile nearly died. She'd seen from the moment he opened the door that his eyes were blue. She just hadn't noticed how the hardness of his face extended to his eyes. They stared back at her, utterly emotionless, revealing nothing.

Cold, she thought distantly as a sudden chill shuddered through her. So cold.

She peered into those eyes, desperately searching for some reassuring sign this was the type of man who might be willing to help her. Some flicker of warmth. Some hint of kindness.

She found none. There was nothing but that cold hardness.

"Nice to meet you," he said, his tone polite and nothing more.

She made some sound of agreement, unable to do anything else but nod.

"Please come in," he said, stepping back from the doorway and gesturing with his arm.

Ducking her head to hide the sudden misgivings she was certain were written all over her face, Karina entered the house, Viktor following close behind.

Luke Hubbard led them into a living room located to the left of the entryway. The room was stylishly furnished, with sleek modern furniture and high-grade electronics, but it was as cold as the man who lived there. She saw no personal items, no photographs anywhere. There were not even any books or newspapers lying about, no sign that anyone had done any actual living here. It appeared to be as sterile as a hotel room.

As they took seats, she and Viktor on the couch across from Luke Hubbard, she tried to remember everything Viktor had told her about this man. He was an attorney, a successful one if his home was any indication. She would have expected as much. He and Viktor had met at Yale, where Sergei had sent Viktor to study. He was a widower, Viktor had said.

As the thought crossed her mind, she automatically lowered her gaze to his hand. His ring finger was bare. It made sense. Viktor hadn't said when the man's wife had died, but Karina had assumed it had been some time ago. It seemed unlikely he would approach a recent widower with his plan, no matter the circumstances. No, the man must have lost his wife at least several years ago, long enough that it was no longer appropriate for him to wear a ring.

Of course, her husband had been dead less than two months, yet she no longer wore his ring. It had seemed wrong to once she'd learned the truth about the kind of man he'd been and discovered just how much trouble he'd left her with. Even if she hadn't, she likely would have had little difficulty removing the ring.

"So what brings you to Baltimore?" Luke Hubbard asked.

Viktor sighed. "We need your help."

"What is it?"

"First I need your word that you will not tell anyone about what we are about to discuss."

"Of course," he said without hesitation, as a true friend would. Karina took some small comfort from the gesture.

Viktor drew in a breath. "In January Karina's husband,

Dmitri, was murdered. He worked for a man named Anton Solokov. I don't know if you're familiar with the name."

Luke Hubbard frowned, his forehead briefly furrowing as he appeared to consider the name. "I don't think so."

"He's one of the wealthiest men in Russia. Like so many others, he moved in swiftly after the fall of the Soviet Union and made his fortune, first with an oil company, then diversifying into minerals."

"Is that where your husband was murdered?" Luke Hubbard asked, turning that cold gaze on Karina. "Russia?"

"Moscow," she confirmed.

"Solokov was responsible," Viktor said.

Luke Hubbard's eyebrows rose the slightest bit. "Responsible," he echoed. "You're saying he had your husband murdered?"

"Yes," she said.

"How do you know?"

"Two men came to our house one night," she said, trying not to shudder at the memory. "I was in the kitchen. Dmitri had just come home when they knocked on the door. He answered. From what I could hear, it was two men. They said that Solokov wanted to see him immediately. He tried to tell them he had just gotten home and they insisted he would have to come with them. The way the man said it made it clear he was threatening Dmitri. Dmitri became very quiet and said, 'He knows, doesn't he?' One of the men said, 'That you've been stealing from him? Yes, he knows.' There was nothing for a second, then a sound like

Dmitri trying to slam the door shut. I heard it crash against the wall, then Dmitri cried out, like he had been hit. I came out of the kitchen to see what had happened. Dmitri was on the floor. His face was bloody and one of the men was trying to pull him up. He saw me and told the other man, 'Take care of her.' The second man started to come toward me. He was reaching into his coat and I thought he might have a gun." She swallowed hard. "I ran before he could catch me and went out the back door. I got away." Leaving Dmitri behind, she thought guiltily.

"Two days later Dmitri was found dead outside the city," Viktor said. "He'd been tortured."

"Did you know your husband was stealing from his boss?" Luke Hubbard asked. It sounded like an accusation.

"No," Karina said firmly. His expression didn't change. She couldn't tell if he believed her.

"There's more," Viktor said. "There have been rumors for a long time that Solokov has connections to organized crime. The mafia. They have never been proven, but most likely only because he has connections with the police, as well."

"You think the Russian mafia is involved?"

"It is possible. If Solokov was laundering money for the mafia, then some of the money he stole might be theirs."

"Do you even have any evidence beyond the comment she overheard that Solokov was involved?"

"Everything else that happened is my evidence."

"What else?"

"My father's death, for one thing," Viktor interjected.

"According to the news, your father fell victim to a drive-by shooting, most likely by gang members who were shooting at someone else."

"A lie," Viktor said, anger darkening his face. "A cover-up to conceal the truth."

"What makes you think this Solokov was involved?"

"Karina contacted my father after Dmitri's death. She has no other family. She knew how powerful Solokov is and didn't know who to trust. Using his diplomatic status, my father arranged for her visa through the embassy and for her to travel to the United States via private jet. He suspected she wasn't safe there. Solokov's reach is too great. But now that my father is dead, her situation has changed."

"How so?"

"Yesterday my visa was revoked," she said. "Without my godfather to intervene, I am being sent home."

"It is Solokov's doing," Viktor said harshly. "He has political connections, as well. Her visa was revoked too quickly to be a coincidence."

"You believe Solokov had your father killed?"

"It certainly makes more sense than him being mistakenly targeted in a drive-by shooting by a random gang member, as your country is suggesting. And he had no other enemies, no reason why anyone else would deliberately kill him. There is only Solokov. As long as Karina was in his home, she was safe from Solokov. He's trying to force her back to Russia, where there is nowhere she can run where he cannot find her."

"For what purpose?"

"He must believe she was aware of what Dmitri was doing. If Dmitri didn't tell him where the money was, then she is his only means of getting it back."

Luke Hubbard nodded. "So you're looking for legal advice? Help with how to stay in the country? That's really not my expertise, but I can certainly recommend some good attorneys who specialize in immigration matters."

Her gaze flicked to Viktor's, reading the same touch of embarrassment in his eyes that she felt rising in her cheeks. It had been his idea, yet now that the moment was here he seemed unwilling to voice it.

"No," Viktor said simply. "That's not why we are here."

In the silence that followed, Luke Hubbard's eyes narrowed, shifting from Viktor to her and back again.

"What exactly *are* you here for?"

So be it, she thought. If anyone should make the request of this complete stranger it should be her. It was her life. She shouldn't rely on anyone else to beg for it.

"Viktor believes the best way for me to remain in this country is to marry a United States citizen."

She lifted her chin and met his cold stare.

"We are here to ask you to marry me."

LUKE HAD YEARS OF EXPERIENCE at schooling his expression to reveal absolutely nothing, but the woman's ridiculous statement nearly managed to crack his composure. It was sheer strength of will that kept him from flinching at her words.

Marriage. Even the idea sent a jolt of pain through

him, the heat of it searing his insides until it felt like he was being burned alive.

Instantly, Melanie's face rose in his mind, the same image that always did. The way she'd looked at her happiest, her head thrown back in laughter, her smile wide, her eyes fixed unerringly, so lovingly, on him and him alone.

The way she'd looked just before she died.

Another sharp pain, harder than the first, shafted through him. He swallowed slowly and blinked the image away, entirely too aware of the two people sitting across from him, watching him intently.

There was only one woman he'd ever wanted to marry, and in the years since her death he'd never once considered taking that step with another. Hell, he'd never been tempted to do so much as let a woman leave a toothbrush in his home. If he had been tempted to take another walk down the aisle, it certainly wouldn't have been with some woman he'd met less than five minutes earlier.

She was pretty in a pale, delicate way. Chin-length black hair. Finely carved features, perhaps sharper than they should have been thanks to what he suspected was an unnatural thinness. Looking closely, he finally noticed the weariness in her eyes. She was young, most likely in her late twenties. Her voice carried a trace of an accent he would have pegged as Eastern European even had he not known where she was from, though her English was impeccable.

"You're proposing a marriage for green-card purposes?" he said coolly.

"It is the best way to keep Karina in the country," Viktor said.

"Surely there are less drastic measures available."

"If there were, we would pursue them. As you said, we have no real evidence that Solokov is responsible for the deaths of Dmitri and my father. And even if we were to pursue other avenues, if we failed and then resorted to marriage it would look suspicious. Better to do it now."

"So you're going straight to the nuclear option?"

"As I said, it is the best way."

"I took an oath to uphold the law. What you're suggesting is illegal."

"So is murder," Viktor shot back. "And the crime is much greater. That is what will happen if Solokov captures her. Once he realizes she knows nothing, he will not hesitate to dispose of her. But that realization will only come after he's done everything he can to learn what he believes she knows."

Even without the raw emotion in the man's voice, there was no missing the implication.

A slight motion at the edge of his vision drew Luke's eye to the woman. She must have shuddered at Viktor's words. Even now she clasped her hands in her lap, her grip so tight her knuckles were white, her head bowed slightly. He could still see her eyes, staring straight in front of her, looking slightly glassy.

He would have liked to believe she'd feigned the reaction. He knew how to read people's expressions well enough to know she had not. The woman was afraid.

Fortunately he'd long since hardened himself against

such displays of emotion, whether hers or Viktor's. He turned his attention back to his supposed friend.

Viktor continued, "Surely a little fraud is minor in comparison to what Solokov intends for her."

"I'm not certain the United States government will see it that way."

"There is no reason it has to know."

"They'll likely want to investigate the validity of the marriage, especially if you're right and someone is pushing to have her deported in the first place. Do you really think two people who've never met would be able to pull that off?"

"You were always quick to learn and Karina is motivated. She cannot go back to Russia. There is no one left we can trust, not fully. There is no family, and Solokov has enough money to be able to buy anyone. At least here in the United States, there is a chance I can protect her."

"You mean *I* can protect her," Luke said. "To make a marriage believable for immigration purposes, we would have to live together, she and I." He turned to find Karina staring at him. If possible, she seemed to have gone even paler. "Are you comfortable with that idea?"

She swallowed, a flicker of emotion he couldn't quite read passing over her eyes. Nervousness? Fear?

But she never blinked, never looked away from his gaze. "I don't want to die."

The words were plain, simply stated. They carried more impact than if she'd accompanied them with tears or a choked sob. Such melodramatic embellishments would have been easily dismissed. But voiced without artifice or manipulation, the basic statement of an elemental human desire was harder to ignore.

That didn't mean he couldn't try. He turned away from those wide, vulnerable eyes.

"Why me?" he asked Viktor, more a demand than a question.

"Because I trust you. There are few people I could say that about."

Luke said nothing, simply stared at the man he'd considered a friend and was no longer sure he should. Would a true friend make such an outlandish request knowing the great personal cost to him? Or was it the sign of a friend that the man would trust him to help this woman?

As expected, it didn't take Viktor long to rush in to fill the silence. "Obviously I know you aren't married and I doubted you would be involved in any kind of relationship that would prevent you from agreeing to help us." He raised his brows, as though prompting Luke to prove him wrong.

Luke tipped his head in acknowledgment. It was hardly a secret he hadn't been involved with anyone seriously since Melanie's death.

"I also knew you would not be able to stand by and watch an innocent woman die when there is something you can do to prevent it."

"Even if that were true, this hardly seems like a situation any sane person would get involved in. People who try to help her don't seem to last long."

"I know we are asking a great deal—" the woman said.

"Yes," he returned coolly. "You are."

She flinched and clamped her mouth shut.

"You're asking me to commit an illegal act, place my entire life and career in jeopardy, and for what? What exactly am I supposed to get out of this?"

Her face flushed to a bright red, and he belatedly realized how that might have sounded. Did she think he was demanding full marital rights if he agreed to be her husband? He almost wondered how she would respond if he were that kind of man. Then again, if he were, he doubted Viktor would have brought her here in the first place.

Indeed, his purported friend hardly seemed to have noticed the possible implication. "You can help an old friend save what's left of his family," Viktor said fervently. "We may not share blood, but you know better than anyone that blood is not a requirement for family. My father thought so, too. He lost his life protecting hers. I can't let his sacrifice be for nothing."

The desperation in the voice of the typically charming, carefree Viktor Yevchenko left no doubt his friend meant every word. For just a moment, Luke felt a small part of himself relent ever so slightly.

The rest of him managed to hold fast. He wasn't about to buy their story without checking into it. He couldn't imagine why an old friend he'd known and trusted for years would come to him with this outlandish proposal unless it were true, but then, the whole situation had been thrown into his lap so suddenly and without warning that he hadn't even had a chance to process it.

"I'll need some time to think about it."

"Think quickly," Viktor said. "Time is one thing we don't have much of."

With a terse nod, Luke rose to his feet, more than ready to remove these two from his home and get to dealing with the troublesome issues they raised. If only he hadn't invited them in to begin with.

Picking up his cue, Viktor and the woman stood, as well.

They made their way back to the door in silence. Luke pulled the door open and waited.

Viktor stopped first before passing through the doorway. "As I said, she is like family to me, Hubbard. You of all people know what it's like to lose family. That's another reason I came to you."

Although he wasn't about to let Viktor see it, the remark hit home, just like the man must have known it would, damn him. "I'll be in touch," Luke said stiffly.

Luke saw Viktor barely manage to tamp down his frustration. With a tight nod, his supposed friend stepped out the door.

And then there was one…

Karina started to follow Viktor, only to stop in front of Luke.

He braced himself for whatever emotional appeal she might offer. The tears. The sobs. None of which would work. He wasn't about to be manipulated.

Instead, she simply met his eyes, her own bleak and tired. "Thank you for your time," she said softly. With that, she moved to join Viktor.

Luke remained where he stood and watched them make their way to the vehicle parked in front of his home. The woman walked with her head up, but her shoulders still seemed to sag, her posture defeated. As though she'd given up. As though she already believed he'd made the decision he damn well should, but somehow hadn't.

Suddenly realizing how long he'd been standing there, he forced himself to close the door. It didn't rid him of the image of that look in her eyes, nor the slump of her shoulders as she walked away.

Troubled, he moved down the hall toward his office. He needed more information. Like it or not, it appeared he had a decision to make.

Even as part of him suspected he'd never had any choice in the matter at all.

Chapter Two

At 6:58 a.m., Luke placed an order for two coffees with the barista at the counter. Two minutes later, he was seated at a table at the front of the coffee shop, two paper cups in front of him, when Darren Jensen walked through the door, on time as always.

He must have spotted Luke through the front window, as intended, because he headed straight toward him without scanning the room first. Jensen was already reaching for one of the cups even before he started to pull out the open chair. "For me?"

"Of course. Thanks for meeting with me."

"It's the least I can do. Anybody who drives in from Baltimore first thing in the morning instead of making do with a phone call is pretty much asking for a face-to-face, don't you think?"

"I had some business in Washington," Luke said mildly. It was the truth. He would have business to attend to, one way or another, whatever Jensen told him.

He watched the man take a long swallow from his

cup, pushing back a twinge of impatience. As would be expected for someone who worked for the government, Jensen's suit was less expensive than Luke's own, but the man was still as immaculately groomed as he'd been when they'd been colleagues at the same law firm years earlier. Pursuing an interest in public service, Jensen had later gone to work for the State Department, making him an excellent source for exactly the kind of answers Luke was looking for. They'd always been on friendly terms, if not outright friends, and remained cordial after Jensen's career change. If it was a friendship, it was the best kind, one where the only favors asked were professional or informational.

Not incredibly personal, he thought, his mind returning to the subject that had occupied his thoughts for nearly twenty-four hours now.

No, he would quite happily do without those kinds of friends.

As soon as Jensen began to lower his cup to the table, Luke spoke. "What do you have for me?"

"Nothing good. Is your firm thinking of doing business with Solokov? Because if you are, I'd think again."

"He's that bad?"

"Men in today's Russia don't stay as rich as Solokov without help from friends in high places and ones in low ones. And these aren't the kind of friends you'd want to get on the wrong side of."

"So he has government connections."

"And mafia ones. Nothing I can prove concretely, but that's what the talk around him indicates, and there's too much there to just be rumors. Like most of the oligarchs who made their fortunes after the fall of the Soviet Union, Solokov knew how to play dirty, and he played to win, with plenty of backing from those friends I mentioned. In today's economy, especially Russia's, many of those Russian billionaires who rose up in the past few decades have lost most, if not all, of their fortunes, especially if they fell out of favor with the government. Not Solokov. He might have taken a hit, but he's still standing."

And if he had taken a hit financially, he would be even more protective of what he had left, Luke deduced. "Which brings us to Dmitri Fedorov."

Jensen nodded. "Formerly of Solokov's employ, currently six feet under. Turned up about a month and a half ago. Murdered."

"Any word who's responsible?"

"None officially. But considering how badly he'd been tortured, it definitely wasn't random. And when a high-level financial manager for a very rich man turns up dead in the condition he was found in, most people are going to be casting a suspicious eye in his boss's direction."

"Including the police?"

Jensen smiled wryly. "I said most people. Solokov has those friends I mentioned. Officially no connection has been made between Fedorov and his former employer. I'm sure the man hasn't even been questioned, not even politely."

"Are there any other reasonable possibilities for why someone would kill Fedorov?"

"There's always the chance he was involved in something unrelated to Solokov, some shady side action that got him killed. There doesn't appear to be any evidence of that, but he could have done that good of a job keeping it under wraps. It's a pretty distant possibility though. The smart money says it was Solokov."

"Why would Solokov have him killed?"

"Not just killed. Tortured. The way my contact described the photographs of Fedorov's body, he had very specifically, very carefully been tortured in a way designed to elicit information, not simply cause pain. Whoever did it to him wanted something from him. Best guess is Fedorov took something he shouldn't have, like large sums of money, which is the only thing he would likely have access to which would be worth taking, and worth getting that upset about."

"What about a business competitor of Solokov? Someone trying to get some information about Solokov or his company by any means necessary."

"From what I gather, they likely would have targeted someone far junior than Fedorov, someone whose death wouldn't make such a splash. If Solokov wasn't involved, then taking out someone so high up in his organization would be risking getting on his bad side, which would probably lead to him bringing in all those friends of his to find out who's responsible. No, whoever did this did so with Solokov's full knowledge and blessing."

"So Fedorov probably managed to take a great deal of money, enough to be worth torturing him over, and Solokov wants it back."

"That's what it looks like. And there might be more to it than simply being pissed off about being taken by someone he trusted. From what my contact told me, the rumors of Solokov's close ties with organized crime are no joke. There's a chance Solokov was working with the mafia's money."

"And it could be the Russian mafia's money that Fedorov stole," Luke said, his unease growing. "No wonder Solokov wanted it back."

"Especially because he wouldn't have been able to tell the mafia he let one of his people steal their money. He would have had to quietly replace it, most likely from his own private fortune, completely separate from the company. That couldn't have been fun."

So far everything Viktor and Karina had told him was lining up, Luke thought, dread beginning to pool in his gut. He'd wanted nothing more than to have Jensen tell him otherwise. He didn't know why Viktor would have lied, especially when the man knew he had the resources to check the story. That hadn't stopped him from spending much of the past day trying to think of a reason. Anything to make it easier to turn down the ridiculous request made by Viktor.

And Karina.

Which brought them to the main topic. "What about Fedorov's wife?"

"I assume you mean his current wife, Karina, since that's the name you gave me on the phone. Karina Andreevna Fedorova. Nearly two decades his junior. They'd been married for five years before his death."

"How old is she now?" Luke asked, the question rising automatically to his tongue. He immediately regretted it. It really wasn't relevant.

"Twenty-eight."

Five years, Luke thought. She'd been so young when she'd married, especially a man so much older. Or maybe that wasn't so unusual in Russia. It was something else he didn't know, which was why he really had no business getting involved in any of this.

Jensen continued, "She worked for an upscale interior designer in Moscow. She left Russia within days of her husband's death, the timing of which probably isn't a coincidence. Most likely she knew what her husband was doing and why he was killed, and knew it was time to get out of dodge. Lucky for her, she had a connection of her own, Sergei Yevchenko, a consul with the Russian embassy in D.C. He arranged to bring her here, and she was staying with him up until his sudden death a week ago." Jensen stopped, his brows going up in silent question. "Which I'm guessing is what brings us here today."

Luke nodded.

"I'm still curious about your interest in this. Yevchenko's murder was certainly highly publicized. A foreign diplomat, especially one from a high-profile country with an always delicate relationship with the U.S., being murdered is big news. But I'm pretty sure neither his goddaughter nor the connection to Solokov was mentioned in the press. Which makes me wonder how you knew about it."

Luke took a slow, deep breath. And so it began. He'd been prepared for this moment, but had hoped to be able to avoid it. If only Jensen had been able to prove Viktor's story a lie, or that what Karina Fedorova faced was not so dire. But here they were.

"I'm involved with her." A lie, the first of many, laying the necessary groundwork if he actually went through with this.

For a moment, Jensen didn't seem to understand, his brow furrowing. "Fedorov's wife?" Luke nodded. "How involved?"

"Very."

Jensen released a low whistle. "You might want to rethink that."

A whisper of a smile played against Luke's mouth. "I might. But some things aren't quite so easy to say no to."

Jensen frowned and gave a little shake of his head. "You know, in all the years I've known you, I don't remember you ever being 'very involved' with a woman."

That was because he hadn't been, not as long as Jensen had known him. "What can I say? I was waiting for the right one. Karina's something special."

"Can't argue with you there. I saw a few pictures. She's quite attractive. But no woman is worth the kind of trouble this one brings with her."

"Is there any evidence Solokov is coming after her, any proof Yevchenko's death is connected to all of this?"

The look Jensen gave him was clearly pitying. "It's not likely to be a coincidence."

"And yet, they happen sometimes."

"Not in this case, they don't. A high-ranking Russian diplomat falling victim to a drive-by shooting is not something that simply happens. No, he was taken out. It takes a lot of hubris to pull something like that, and from what I hear, that's one thing Solokov isn't lacking."

"So what will happen to her?"

"The way I hear it, she's due to be sent back to Russia ASAP."

"Which is what Solokov wants."

"I imagine. He wouldn't have gone to this much trouble if he didn't. He must think she was involved with her husband's theft, and either has the money or knows where it is. It makes sense, considering she knew to run."

Or she was there when Solokov's men came for her husband and barely managed to escape herself, Luke thought. But of course, there was no way for Jensen or anyone else to know that.

"Is there any chance she'll be able to protect herself from Solokov if she's sent back?"

A hint of sympathy flashed across Jensen's face. "Doesn't look like it. She may be a thief like her husband, but we're not talking about someone with the background or the connections to go head-to-head with Solokov. She's an interior decorator. She finds pretty things to fill the homes of rich people. Some of those rich people might be able to help her, but even if they could, what happened to her godfather would probably give them second thoughts."

"There's no chance our government will grant her some kind of asylum?"

"On what grounds? She's not a target of political persecution, at least not in any way that would qualify. Besides, a Russian diplomat was murdered on American soil. The U.S. government is not about to interfere with anything the Russians want at the moment, and right now, they want her shipped back to Moscow."

"Where she'll be completely at Solokov's mercy."

Jensen's eyes grew shrewd. "No doubt. Something I'm sure she knows, too. Which may be why she became involved with you. Maybe she's looking for someone to marry her so she can stay in the country."

"She's not like that," Luke said automatically, somehow managing to keep the irony out of his tone.

"She's not, huh? Then why do I get the feeling you knew most of this before I told you? Was it because she told you? Maybe she already asked you to marry her to save her. Or is that an idea you came up with on your own because you want to save her since you're so 'very involved'?"

With practiced ease, Luke let the words bounce off him, not letting a single muscle twitch or blink of the eye give the slightest indication Jensen's comments had hit home. Odd to think that Jensen was right, and yet hadn't even managed to come up with the real way this had all come about. That was how outlandish it was.

Luke shot the man a wry smile. "Does that sound like something I would do?"

He waited to see how the man would respond, a test run of how someone who knew him would react to the idea.

For a long moment, Jensen simply looked at him, his eyes assessing, his expression considering.

Luke simply stared back.

Then Jensen's expression eased, his lips working into a smile of his own. "No, I guess not. But that doesn't mean she hasn't thought of it."

"I told you, she's not like that."

"Uh-huh," Jensen said into his coffee cup, his disbelief coming across loud and clear despite the muffled sound. "But seriously, you need to rethink your involvement with this woman. No good can come of it. Trust me, you do not want to be involved in this."

No, Luke agreed silently, his heart sinking, he didn't. Unfortunately, he already was.

The biggest question was why. The world was full of sad stories and people in desperate situations. All he had to do was watch five minutes of the news to see them every day. He'd never been remotely inspired to come to the aid of any of them. But now he was faced with this woman, asking something that wasn't in any way reasonable for one person to ask of another.

And the "no" that should rise to his tongue so easily failed to come.

Perhaps it was because the problem had been so directly laid at his feet. There wasn't a question of what might happen or the possibility that someone else might pick up the ball and run with it if he failed to. Viktor had brought the situation to him and laid it out in a way that left him little choice.

If you don't do this, she will die.

It shouldn't matter. He shouldn't care about her. He still didn't really. But that didn't mean he could live with this woman's death on his hands. Didn't mean he could stand by and essentially kill the last member of Viktor's family.

"You know better than anyone that blood is not a requirement for family."

As much as he didn't want to be involved, as much as he wanted to say no, as much as it would surprise anyone who thought they knew him, it seemed he wasn't quite cold enough to allow that to happen.

THE SOUND OF THE DOORBELL came out of nowhere, the noise loud and jarring, scraping against Karina's already-raw nerves. Seated on the couch in Viktor's living room, she sent a nervous glance toward the hall to the entryway. She knew there was little chance Solokov's people would come right up to the front door and ring the bell, but there were other threats that might. Threats that seemed even more imminent at the moment. Government officials. Immigration officers there to send her home.

To Russia.

To Solokov.

She waited nervously as Viktor made his way to the door, waited for his reaction to whatever he found there.

"It's Luke," he said, no doubt for her benefit, before she heard him open the door.

The announcement did nothing to reassure her. Instead, it only served to intensify the tension gripping

her insides. She'd barely slept last night, the cold, unyielding face of a stranger looming too large in her
mind. She and Viktor had both been waiting for a tele-
phone call, expecting Luke Hubbard to deliver his
answer that way. She didn't know what it meant that
he'd instead chosen to come here himself, a mere day
after hearing their request. Did it mean he'd decided to
do it, or that he'd simply come to deliver the bad news
himself, having the courtesy of telling them in person?
What did it mean that he'd chosen so fast? And what
answer did she really want to hear?

Karina rose slowly from her seat, feeling not as
though she were about to face an attorney, but a judge,
one prepared to deliver his decision to her fate.

Luke Hubbard stepped into the room first, his eyes
immediately finding hers. He said nothing, simply
stared at her. She searched his expression for some sign
of what had brought him here, what his decision was.
He remained as unreadable as she remembered, his eyes
cold as ever.

Viktor moved into the room behind him. "Well?"
he prompted.

"I want to make a few things clear first."

She frowned uncertainly. "Okay."

"You have to agree that as soon as the danger to your
life is over, we will terminate the marriage."

He's agreeing to the marriage, she thought, the shock
so severe she merely felt numb from it. There was no
room for relief, or unease, or anything else. The shock
was too great.

"Of course," Viktor said when she didn't respond.

"I need to hear it from her," Luke said, never taking his eyes off her.

"Yes," she made herself say. "I agree."

"You'll sign a prenuptial agreement." He reached into his coat and pulled out a large brown envelope. "Naturally you should read it first. It guarantees that when the marriage ends, we will each leave it with only what we brought into it."

He held out the document to her. She accepted it, scanning over the words on the first page without really seeing them. It hardly mattered what it said. She was only bringing one thing to the marriage and it was all she wanted from it. Her life. To live.

"Of course."

"You'll have to move into my house immediately after the ceremony to make it believable."

"I know." It was as they'd discussed.

For a long moment, he simply stared at her again, saying nothing. She wondered if he was changing his mind. He hadn't agreed yet, not really.

She held her breath, not certain what she wanted him to say next.

He nodded sharply. "Then let's do this."

Karina barely had time to react when Viktor clapped his hands. "Good. Now that that's settled, we can't waste any more time."

"Agreed. We'll need wedding rings."

"Done," Viktor said, surprising her. She watched him move to a nearby desk and retrieve two small boxes. He flipped them open, showing the contents to her and Luke. A plain gold band and another with a small but lovely diamond.

"Were you that positive I would agree or did you have someone else to ask if I didn't?" Luke asked.

"I thought it best to be prepared for anything," Viktor said. "We don't have any time to waste."

"Agreed," Luke said. "We'll do this today."

"Today?" Karina echoed, eyes wide. Even Viktor seemed surprised.

Luke shot her a glance. "Is there a reason to wait?"

"No." Of course there wasn't. It was just happening so fast. Two minutes ago she hadn't even known his answer. Now they would be married today, perhaps within hours.

"There's no waiting period to be married in Virginia," he said. "With any luck, we should be able to find a chapel where we can have the ceremony. I'll call my assistant and have her find one. She can call us on the way with the information. It would look better if we did that rather than have it done at a courthouse or a justice of the peace. The marriage might seem more genuine if we went to all that trouble to be married in a religious setting."

"Good idea," Viktor said.

"Should we go?" Luke asked, looking solely at her. And it occurred to her that, in a way, he was now asking her to marry him.

Her earlier doubts about whether she could go through with this even if he agreed came back in a rush. If she wanted to stop this, now would be the time to do it.

Agreeing to this would mean placing her life in this

man's hands. She'd done it with Sergei, and to a lesser degree Viktor. But they were practically family. This man was a stranger. A man she knew nothing about but the little Viktor had told her. Including the fact that Viktor trusted him. Was that enough?

But it wasn't as though she could turn back now. It was she who had asked him. And there were no other options available to her. This was her only chance. The stranger or certain death.

So why did the choices seem equally perilous?

She forced herself to swallow, to lift her head and keep every trace of doubt from her face.

"Yes," she said.

And with that, her future was secure.

For now.

Chapter Three

"I do."

Karina knew she had said the words. She had felt them rising in her throat, felt herself moving her lips to form them while keeping the smile on her face. But even as they came out in her own voice, it seemed as though someone else was saying them, as though this was happening to another person.

For the past few months, her life had taken on an unreal feeling. Her desperate flight to the United States. Sergei's death. Viktor's crazy idea. But nothing had seemed less real than this, standing before a minister and marrying a man she didn't know.

What am I doing? The question echoed over and over in her head with increasing desperation.

Surviving, a hard voice in the back of her mind hissed.

In the wake of her declaration, the minister continued speaking. She barely heard him as she stared up into the eyes of the man before her.

Luke Hubbard.

The man she was marrying.

The hard lines of his face were eased into a softer expression, the corners of his mouth turned upward slightly in the closest thing she'd seen to a smile from him. Anyone else looking at him might see exactly what they were meant to, a man deeply in love, gazing at his bride with tenderness, unable to take his eyes off her.

But she alone stared into his eyes, and in them she saw the truth.

There was no love there, no feeling.

There was nothing at all.

She had no reason to expect otherwise. It was all she'd received from this man from the moment they'd met, and it hadn't changed the slightest since he'd shocked her by agreeing to Viktor's proposal. She knew better than anyone else exactly why they were standing here, why they were doing this, and it had nothing to do with love. This was a simple arrangement, nothing else.

But to stand there before God and make promises neither of them believed or intended to keep, seemed wrong, regardless of the reasons.

The law would not understand. Would God?

If this plan failed and Solokov won, she might be able to ask Him soon enough, she thought, barely suppressing a shudder.

"I do," Luke said, his voice deep and sure, as he continued to peer straight into her eyes.

Karina searched his gaze for any hint of the doubts she was feeling. Of course she found none. There was only the same lack of emotion that sent another chill down her spine.

Then he was reaching for her hand, his fingers long and warm as they lifted her own cold, numb ones and slid the ring Viktor had provided onto the one where it belonged. Her breath hitched in her throat as she tracked the band's progress until it reached the end of her finger. Seeing it there somehow made it so much more real.

She might have continued staring at it if he hadn't suddenly released her hand. Viktor pressed the other ring into it. She quickly placed it on the hand Luke held up, doing her best to keep the contact between them as minimal as possible, releasing his fingers as soon as the band was in place.

She swallowed. There. It was done.

She was so consumed with relief that she barely heard what the minister was saying.

"…I now declare you husband and wife."

It took a moment for the words to sink in. Karina sent a startled glance at the minister, who beamed at them each in turn. Then he looked to Luke.

"You may kiss your bride."

Her gaze flew to Luke's. His smile deepened. And for the first time she saw something else flickering in his steady gaze. Something that sent a jolt through her system and suddenly made her very nervous.

He started to lean forward. She forced herself to relax, to smile, as though she wanted this, the way she was supposed to. Her eyes drifted shut automatically and she felt a twinge of relief push past her nervousness. She'd known this was coming and knew how important it was for it to be convincing. At least she wouldn't have to look at him, could pretend he was someone else. Not a man with cold eyes who felt nothing for her.

She somehow wasn't prepared for the instant when his lips met hers. Another jolt shot through her at the connection. Her mouth fell open on its own as his moved against it. The first caress was brief, experimental. The second immediately deepened the kiss, his lips firm and strong and sure. The man knew how to kiss. She recognized that instinctively, even as the fervor, the intensity, of it caught her by surprise in spite of everything.

She felt his arms go around her, pulling her up against his body. He pinned her against him, her breasts tight against the wall of his chest, causing her to gasp. He took advantage of the indrawn breath, plunging his tongue into her mouth in one long, confident stroke. She grabbed the front of his shirt and held on tightly, needing to hold on to something solid, feeling strangely as though she were drowning.

Part of her wondered, as though from far, far away, if it was necessary. Would the onlookers really know if he wasn't quite so thorough in his ministrations?

The rest could only respond in kind. Behind the closed lids, her eyes rolled back as she let the wave of sensations—his arms, his chest, his lips, his tongue—carry her away, washing away everything she'd lived with for the past few months. There was only this man. This kiss.

Then it was over. She realized it several seconds after

it actually happened, after he'd broken the connection between their mouths and started to pull away. The two fistfuls of his shirt she gripped prevented him from stepping back entirely.

Her eyes fluttered open. She found herself peering into his. They no longer seemed cold. Instead, they flared with that strange…something.

"Some things should be left until you're alone," she heard Viktor chide, a slightly annoyed note in his voice.

"I think it's lovely," the minister's secretary said.

Karina watched Luke turn to face the minister and his secretary, his smile deepening as he extended his hand to the former.

Still slightly off-balance, she turned to do the same, forcing her mouth to curve upward. They were smiling at her, the expressions on their faces making her feel even more like a liar.

This is not real, she almost wanted to tell them. *Don't be happy for us.*

But she simply lowered her eyes rather than look at their joyous expressions, letting them take the color filling her cheeks for embarrassment, as she tried to calm her suddenly racing heart and understand exactly why a pretend kiss had felt so amazingly real.

"WE'LL NEED TO FILE paperwork with Immigration to inform them of the marriage," Luke murmured low so only she and Viktor could hear as the three of them made their way out of the chapel.

"Should we do that today?" Viktor asked.

Luke shook his head. "My concern is that it would look too suspicious, as though the marriage was strictly for the purposes of keeping her in the country. A couple involved in a whirlwind romance wouldn't be thinking about that on their wedding day. The morning should be fine."

Viktor made a sound of agreement. Karina listened silently, much as she had for most of the day. Strange how she'd had so little input in her own fate. Ever since this nightmare had begun, it seemed like she'd been caught up in events larger than herself, placing her life in the hands of others. First Sergei, then Viktor. Now a stranger. Even now it seemed as though the men had placed themselves in a way so that they could converse without her, with Viktor closest to the street, Luke in the middle and her trailing along on the other side.

The feeling of helplessness chafed, but she didn't know what else she could do. It may be her life, but they knew more about these matters than she did.

They were almost to the parking lot next to the building when Karina spotted a black sedan pulling away from the curb on the street up ahead of them. It began to drive down the street in their direction.

She wasn't certain at first why she noticed it. There was nothing unusual about it. Its make and model were unremarkable. It might have been the strangeness of seeing it there, parked on the street when no other cars were on this quiet stretch of road. It might have been that its windows were a little too dark, tinted to hide its occupants.

Then she realized how slowly it was driving, crawling along on the street far less quickly than it should be.

And she knew exactly what was about to happen, even before she saw the passenger-side window was down.

She opened her mouth to scream, to shout a warning, to do something for once, even as she saw the tiny barrel of a gun emerge from the window.

"No!"

The word was barely out before something large and heavy crashed into her, throwing her down to the ground. The impact knocked the breath from her lungs. A few muffled pops reached her ears. She saw a blur out of the right side of her vision, the side closer to the street, where Viktor was standing.

She whipped her head to look at him.

In time to see him fall to the ground, his face clenched in pain.

For a moment, she could only stare, frozen in disbelief, as past and present blurred, what she was seeing and what she'd only seen in her nightmares blending into one. Viktor's face faded into another, so similar. Sergei. On the ground. Shot.

And then it was Viktor again. Here. Now. Shot.

She lunged forward, only to find her progress impeded by the heavy weight on top of her, holding her back.

"Don't be stupid," a harsh voice said in her ear. Luke.

"I have to help him!" she screamed, struggling to get away.

He tightened his hold in response to her thrashing. "You can't help him! All you can do is get yourself killed."

Even as she heard the words, she felt herself being hauled to her feet and pulled backward. They'd reached the parking lot. There were only four cars in it. He dragged her behind the nearest one, blocking them from the street.

"What are you doing?" she gasped, unable to believe what was happening.

"I'm getting you out of here."

"No! I cannot leave him!"

"My responsibility is to keep anything from happening to you. That's what this was all about, wasn't it?"

"Nothing will happen to me! They're gone!"

"They could double back."

"They won't kill me here!"

"Do you know that for a fact? Do you know with absolute certainty that they won't shoot you, too, just for the hell of it?"

Karina threw her mouth open to say yes. Nothing came out. She couldn't think, couldn't begin to form words. She wanted to scream at him again that she didn't know anything, she hadn't known anything with absolute certainty since this nightmare had begun and everything had started to seem unreal. Like this.

Luke took advantage of her speechlessness to lift her clear off her feet. As soon as she realized what he was doing, she began to struggle anew.

"Don't throw away everything he did for you," Luke said. "Don't make it worth nothing."

The angry words made her go still, torn between what he was saying and what she knew to be right. She couldn't just leave Viktor there, lying on the sidewalk. But what if she was shot? The loss of her own life seemed insignificant compared to what it would mean to Viktor. And this man? If he were shot trying to save her—and she did know they wouldn't hesitate to kill him—then what had all this been for? What had Sergei and Viktor, and perhaps even this man, died for? She did not need another death on her hands. Someone else dead, because of her.

Then they were at his car. Luke yanked the passenger-side door open without stopping and practically hurled her inside. "Stay here and keep your head down." Without waiting for a response, he slammed the door shut in her face.

Ducking her head slightly, she never took her eyes off him as he made his way back to Viktor.

She swiped a trembling hand across her face to wipe away the tears she knew had to be there, only to have her fingers come away dry. She stared at them, disturbed by the sight. It made no sense. Her throat was still raw from begging him not to make her leave Viktor. Her heart felt as though it had been ripped from her chest. How could she not be crying?

She remembered sobbing for Sergei when the news of his death had truly hit her, the tears coming before she realized they were there. Yet now she had none.

A kind of grim understanding fell over her, and with it a fresh stab of pain.

So this is what it is to have no tears left.

The glimmer of something else forced her eyes to refocus. It was the diamond of her wedding ring, sparkling through the gaps between her fingers. She turned her hand over and stared at it, stunned anew.

Her wedding ring.

The ceremony had been less than an hour ago, what now seemed like a lifetime. She'd nearly forgotten.

Karina slowly lifted her head and focused on the man outside her window, ducking low, scanning the street for any sign of the car.

If Viktor was gone, this man was the only person she had left in the world. This stranger.

Her husband.

Chapter Four

Luke never took his eyes off the street as he made his way back to where he'd been forced to leave Viktor, crouching low and remaining behind the few cars in the parking lot as long as he could. Despite the scenario he'd presented to Karina, the street remained empty, with no sign the shooters were doubling back. Evidently they'd chosen the same method they'd used when they killed Viktor's father, driving by and leaving the scene as soon as possible, perhaps feeling all they needed was to get rid of anyone who was helping Karina. Taking her would be just as easy to do later.

Luke gritted his teeth, unable to completely fight back the wave of anger.

It wasn't going to happen. Not as long as he had anything to say about it. They weren't going to succeed, weren't going to get away with this.

By the time he reached the car parked closest to the building, he was reasonably convinced it was safe. He peered around the hood, looking for Viktor.

A groan reached his ears, the sound immediately sending a jolt of relief through him.

He finally darted out into the open. Viktor was on his back on the pavement, but was already pushing himself up on one arm. Luke saw immediately why he didn't use both. The opposite shoulder was dark and wet, the color almost unnoticeable against the black of Viktor's suit jacket, the texture unmistakable. Blood.

Still keeping one eye on the street, Luke moved to his friend's side. "Viktor," he said. "How bad is it?"

"Could be worse," Viktor grimaced. "I am not dead." He looked up, met Luke's eyes, then glanced around him. "Karina?"

"Safe. I got her to the car."

Viktor nodded, a small sigh wheezing from between his teeth. "Good," he said, as Luke had known he would. "Let's get out of here."

He started to shift to his feet. Luke went to take Viktor's good arm. "Come on. We have to get you to a hospital."

"No," Viktor said fiercely, jerking out of his grasp. "No hospital. It's not worth it. Do you really want to have to answer questions about this? Explain to Immigration about the shooting that took place after your wedding? That will certainly raise questions about the circumstances of the marriage, don't you think?" Before Luke could respond, he started walking back to the car.

"We'll have to answer questions anyway when the police start asking them."

"Which they won't do if we don't report it."

"Somebody will."

Viktor glanced quickly around them, his expression incredulous. "Who?"

Luke followed his gaze. The man was right. The chapel was located in a quiet suburban neighborhood. The street remained empty. On the other side of the street was an empty lot, so no witnesses there. No one had come out of the chapel to see what had happened. He glanced at the building. None of the curtains in the windows shifted. There was no sign anyone had noticed and was looking out to monitor the situation. Which meant no one had likely notified the authorities, either. The quiet street remained as much so as when they'd first arrived, as though nothing had happened here at all.

Even so, Luke shook his head. "You've been shot. You need to have that looked at."

"Just take me home. I can make it back to Washington. I know someone I can call to take care of this. We just need to get out of here."

"And if you don't make it back to Washington?"

"It's not that bad," Viktor scoffed. "A graze."

"You know that from all the many times you've been shot?"

"We can't remain in public," Viktor insisted. "We are both targets now, both of us. Remaining in public makes us visible ones, especially if they follow us to the hospital."

"They're long gone."

"You don't know that. And they followed us here, didn't they?"

Luke couldn't argue with that. It was the only way anyone could have found them. He hadn't paid much attention to anyone behind them on the drive here, spending half of the trip on the phone with his assistant, partly getting directions, partly assuring her he really was getting married. Once her disbelief had faded, he'd heard the hurt in her voice, no doubt because she was finding out so late and wasn't invited. He was going to have to do some work to get back on her good side.

It only served to remind him how rushed this had been, how he'd allowed himself to get caught up in the emotion of the story Viktor and Karina had sold him. He was going to have to pay more attention to these things. Of course they would have been watching Viktor's place. Of course they would have followed when they saw the three of them leave. Granted, neither Viktor nor Karina had seemed to think of it, either. But then, they'd all had other things on their mind.

It wasn't a mistake he would make again. Viktor was right. They couldn't remain in the open. Like they were now.

He automatically shot another glance at the street. Still empty. "All right," he said. "Let's go. But we're taking a look at that shoulder in the car. I want to know how bad it is."

Viktor made a vague head gesture, not quite a shake, not quite a nod, that gave no indication of whether he truly agreed. Either way, they started back toward Luke's car.

They'd gone only two steps before Viktor grabbed Luke's arm. "Luke."

Luke stopped and met Viktor's eyes, caught as much by the renewed urgency in his voice as the hand on his arm.

"You understand now how dangerous Solokov is, don't you?" Viktor said, a glowing intensity in his eyes.

"I never had any doubt." Certainly never would have gone through with this if he had.

"You have to keep her safe." He sent an almost reluctant glance at his shoulder. "I don't know if I'm going to be as much help as I wanted to be, so it's up to you. You have to keep her safe. Otherwise, all of this was for nothing."

All of this, Luke thought. Such a simple way to describe so much trouble. The murder of Sergei Yevchenko. Viktor's shooting. His own sudden marriage.

All of this because of one woman.

He glanced toward the car. They'd come close enough that he could see Karina there in the front seat, staring at them intently through the passenger-side window. She looked on the verge of launching herself from the car, her hands pressed against the glass, her face contorted with emotion. Fear. Worry.

Or guilt?

He remembered Jensen's supposition, that Karina had fled Russia because she'd known what her husband was doing and knew Solokov would be coming after her. At the time he'd dismissed it, thinking he knew something Jensen didn't. But did he? Jensen didn't really know the woman, but neither did he.

All of this. Because of her.

"Luke?"

He glanced back to find Viktor watching him, still waiting for a response to what he'd said.

He nodded shortly. "Don't worry. I won't let her out of my sight."

VIKTOR WAS NOT DEAD. It should have been a comfort, but it really wasn't.

He had still been shot, been hurt.

Because of her.

Karina sat silently in Luke's living room, her arms wrapped tightly around herself. She still couldn't believe they hadn't taken Viktor to a hospital. Instead, he had called someone on his mobile phone as they drove back to Washington. A woman Karina had never seen before had been waiting at his building when they dropped him off. He'd said this woman could take care of his injury. Karina had wanted to go inside, reassure herself that he was all right, convince him to go to a doctor if necessary.

Instead, he had simply gotten out of the car, insisting that she go with Luke Hubbard.

And now she was. With him. Alone.

At the sound of footsteps, Karina raised her head in time to see Luke move into the entryway. He stopped there and simply looked at her, his expression remote as ever. He hadn't said anything to her since they'd left Viktor. They'd driven back to Baltimore, back to his house, in silence.

She stared at him, uncertain what to say. She longed for a comforting word, a kind gesture, some token attempt to make her feel better and try to forget about what had happened. It would not work, but at least it would be something. But she already knew better than to expect anything like that from this man.

Suddenly he lurched forward and stalked across the room. "We need to talk."

As expected, there was no kindness in the words. In fact, they seemed as cold as anything he'd ever said to her. He came to a stop in front of her and loomed over her, forcing her to tilt her head back almost painfully to meet his eyes. She straightened in her seat and leaned back to try to ease the pressure. It still felt as though he were towering over her, an intimidating feeling she didn't like. "Okay," she said warily.

"I want to know the truth."

She blinked, confused. "What do you mean?"

"Do you have what Solokov is after? Do you know where the money is?"

His words, spat in quick succession like bullets, blindsided her. She gaped up at him, almost incapable of responding. "I told you I do not."

"Tell me again. Tell me until I believe it."

"You did not believe me before?"

"No," he said so quickly she flinched at the shock of it. "I believed Viktor. He vouched for you. But Viktor's not here right now, and I want to know if you know anything that would have prevented that."

"No!" she said just as fast as he had, but with far more emotion, unable to keep a tremulous note from creeping into the word. "Don't you think I would have said something by now if I knew anything, at least after Sergei's death if I hadn't before?"

"I don't know what you'd do. I don't know *you*."

"Why wouldn't I have said something?"

"Maybe you do know where the money is. Maybe you're just lying low until you think it's safer for you to access it. Maybe that's why you were so willing to sign the prenup. Because you really don't need it, with all that money you have waiting for you once this is all over."

"No!" She threw her hands up as though to ward off his words and gave her head a desperate shake. "It's not true. I swear to you I knew nothing about what Dmitri was doing. I do not know where the money is. If I did I would give it back and put an end to all of this."

"You would give back the kind of money somebody is willing to kill for?"

"It is not worth losing my life."

"If you did give it back, it would make it look like you were involved all along. Solokov would most likely still kill you as punishment. You could know that, figure you might as well keep it if that's the case."

"I don't know anything about the money. I never did."

He surveyed her for a long moment. Was he wondering if she was a good enough actress to lie to him convincingly? Or if she truly could be so stupid that she'd had no idea what her husband had been doing? She almost didn't know which she would like him to believe more.

A familiar wave of humiliation washed over her and she felt heat burn her face. Because as appalling as it was, she really had been that stupid. Not a day had passed since this all began that she hadn't been forced to face the depth of her foolishness. She'd been married to a thief, a criminal. She'd had no idea the kind of man he truly was.

She wanted to believe he hadn't been a criminal when they'd married, that something had changed him over the years.

It was a slightly comforting idea, but also, she suspected, a foolish one.

"All right," Luke said finally. "I believe you."

The words should have offered relief, except that his tone said something else entirely.

She narrowed her eyes on his face. "You do?"

"Yes," he said simply, without hesitation, without inflection.

"That's it?"

"Unless you want to change my mind."

Staring into that hard face, it was impossible to believe anyone could influence this man's thoughts in any way.

"No," she said. "I do not know where the money is." She swallowed hard. "But I could have prevented what happened today."

It hardly seemed possible, but his expression sharpened. "How?"

"I should not have involved him or Sergei in this. Sergei would be alive. Viktor would not have been hurt."

"They wanted to help you, to protect you."

"So that I could live," she said, unable to keep a trace of self-contempt from her voice.

"Nobody wants to die."

"Is my life worth so much more than theirs?" Exhaling sharply, she shook her head. "I am no better than Dmitri."

"What do you mean?"

"He stole from Solokov, not caring what it would mean to anyone but himself. He must have known his theft would be discovered. I am certain he intended to be far away before it happened. He had to know Solokov would not let such a thing go unpunished. He must have made plans to flee the country and go somewhere he could not be found with all that money. And I am also certain his plans did not include me. He would have left me behind, knowing that Solokov would come after me to find out what I knew about what he had done, knowing that he would likely kill me. And I am certain he did not care."

"Except you care about what happened to Viktor and his father. You're nothing like your husband."

"I cared too late. I should have thought about the danger to other people before I contacted Sergei. But I only thought of myself, like Dmitri. How I did not want to die."

And instead Sergei had died. Viktor might have. And this man—

She raised her eyes to his face as a sudden fear struck her. She did not even know this man, yet he had tried to help her. And he could die for it. For her.

No.

She stood abruptly. "I should go."

"What are you talking about?"

"This was a mistake. I should not have involved you. I'm sorry."

"So now you're going to go?"

She nodded fiercely, determination surging through her. "If anything happens to you…" The nod quickly changed to a sharp shake of her head. "No, I cannot let anyone else be hurt for me."

"Where exactly are you going to go? You say you don't have Solokov's money. Do you even have any at all?"

Yes, she wanted to protest. She did have some. But not the kind he was talking about, the kind she would need to live on, to escape, to survive. She had only the little she'd managed to withdraw from her bank account immediately after Dmitri's death. She would need help accessing her account back home.

The sense of helplessness washed over her once more. She was completely at the mercy of the generosity of others.

"I didn't think so," he said. "And even if you did, I put myself on the line. After dragging me into this situation, you'd really walk away and destroy my life just like that?"

Her eyes flared in surprise. Even as she struggled to absorb the words, he stepped forward, moving close. Too close. She could almost feel the heat of his body. Or maybe it was the sheer intensity of his fierce stare. "What do you mean?"

"What do you think the government's going to think when my new bride suddenly disappears? How do you think that's going to make me look?"

"You can say I tricked you."

"I'd look like a fool."

"It is better than being dead."

"Is it? I could go to jail. I could be disbarred. I violated the law I took a vow to uphold. I could lose everything."

"I did not intend for any of that to happen," she said weakly.

"You should have thought about that before you forced me into this."

She gaped at him. "No one forced you into anything. I *asked*. Viktor and I—we both asked. You had a choice."

"No, I didn't. Maybe you knew that, maybe you didn't. But Viktor did. That's why he brought you here."

"What are you talking about?"

He stared at her for a long moment, his face practically in hers, so close she could see every ring of color in his eyes. Then he abruptly turned away. "Forget it."

She watched him stalk across the room, coming to a stop in front of the window. He folded his arms over his chest and stared out into the growing twilight.

"Why *did* you agree?"

It was the question she'd wanted to ask from the moment he'd informed her and Viktor of his decision, but had been afraid to until now, afraid that he would change his mind if forced to assess his reasons. But now it was done, as he'd told her.

"I had my reasons."

Suddenly a terrible idea came to mind, one which placed his earlier question in a different light. As soon as she thought it, a cold certainty took hold, sending a sick feeling through her body.

"Was it for the money?"

His head snapped up. "What?"

"Is that why you married me? The real reason you are asking about it now? Because you thought I knew where the money was and you could force me to tell you once we were alone?" It made too much sense not to be a possibility, certainly more than any other she could think of.

He didn't respond at first, simply staring at her, his gaze so unrelenting she had to fight the urge to tear hers away. She couldn't yield, couldn't let him intimidate her, no matter how effective his technique. The answer mattered too much.

Finally he spoke. "You have a strange way of showing gratitude to someone who did you one hell of a favor."

"I think that depends on the reason you did the favor."

One eyebrow arched upward. He gestured toward the room. "Does it look like I need the money?"

She nearly shivered at the deadly calm in his low-pitched voice. "Things are not always what they look like. And for some people there is never enough money."

"Then I'll say it outright. I neither need nor want the money. That's not why I married you."

"So why did you agree? Was it out of kindness? Compassion?" She couldn't keep the skepticism from her tone.

"You don't think I'm capable of either?"

"You do not seem like a man to make decisions based on his emotions."

"And what kind of man do I seem like?"

"A man who would not," she said simply, biting back a stronger answer.

"I guess that proves how little we know each other."

"As you said, you do not know me, and I do not know you. And you still have not answered the question."

He exhaled slowly. She wondered if he was trying to think of a way not to answer, or if he would lie.

Finally he spoke. "I did it for Viktor. He's been a good friend to me over the years, in many ways a better one than I may have deserved."

She could believe that. He didn't look like a man who had friends. Who could be friends with a man as cold as ice? Only someone as charming as Viktor, she supposed, who could be friends with anyone.

He continued. "Like he said, I didn't want to see him lose what's left of his family. I know what that's like." The last words were added almost like an afterthought.

"Because of your wife?" she said without thinking.

In an instant something changed. His eyes narrowed, his expression tightened. "What do you know about my wife?" he barked at her.

The sharpness in his voice startled her. "O-only that she died. Viktor told me."

"What else did he tell you?"

"Nothing," she said quickly, the answer as fast as the question. "Not even her name."

That seemed to take the force out of his sudden anger. He exhaled sharply, his shoulders sagging slightly. "Melanie," he said, not looking at her. "Her name was Melanie."

"That is a nice name," she said stupidly after a moment, trying to fill the sudden silence and not knowing what else to say.

"Yes, well, she was very nice."

For a moment she was tempted to ask what a nice woman had been doing with him. But something in his tone of voice, something in the slump of his shoulders, caused the words to die on her tongue. It was something she'd never heard, never seen from him before, a hint of emotion emerging from beneath his usual coolness. He almost seemed vulnerable, something she never would have thought possible from this man in the short time she'd known him.

She remembered the exchange he and Viktor had shared yesterday. When choosing a man to approach to marry her, Viktor had looked for someone he knew would not be involved with anyone else. He'd known that about this man. Luke Hubbard's wife must have been dead for years, yet there was no chance he would be involved with another woman.

He must have loved her very much, Karina thought faintly. Envy, sharp and painful, stabbed at her. She did her best to swallow the feeling before it pierced too deeply. What must it be like to be so loved by someone that he would continue to mourn her so long after she was gone? Dmitri certainly had not loved her so greatly. He'd plotted to leave her behind to face the consequences of his actions alone, likely knowing her death would be the result, and she couldn't imagine he would have given her a second thought.

Karina was so lost in her own thoughts that she didn't notice Luke's cool mask had fallen back into place until he began speaking again.

"I looked into your situation after you and Viktor came to see me, made some inquiries with some people I know who can find out such things. I wanted to explore the possibility of finding another way for you to remain in the country, one that involved less drastic measures."

"You must not have found one."

"No. I heard that this was a situation no one in the government would come close to touching. If your country wanted to send you back, the U.S. government wasn't going to stand in the way. A Russian diplomat was murdered on U.S. soil. The United States wasn't about to pick a fight with your country over the fate of one woman."

"Of course." She didn't think her life was worth Sergei or Viktor or this man losing theirs. What could it possibly matter compared to the complex relations of whole nations? "Won't your questions make this person suspicious about the reasons for our marriage?"

"I think the circumstances themselves are enough to make anyone with a brain suspicious about the reasons for our marriage." One corner of his mouth curled sardonically. "I made it clear the reason I was asking was because I was interested in you on a personal level."

"Did this person believe you?"

"I think so. As he put it, you're quite attractive."

She had no idea how to respond to that. She wondered what he had said when the man had told him that. She wondered if he agreed.

She wondered why it mattered, why she even cared.

When she said nothing, he continued. "Of course what will really make people suspicious is if you suddenly take off and leave me with a bunch of questions to deal with. Can you promise me you won't do that?"

She hesitated, still unsure he was right. She forced herself to nod. "Yes."

"Good. Now if we're going to make this work, we're going to have to get our stories straight. It's the only way we'll ever convince anybody this is real. Why don't we eat something and we can talk about it?"

She nodded again. Seemingly satisfied, he moved back toward the door and disappeared down the hall, most likely to wherever the kitchen was.

As soon as he was gone, she sighed heavily, releasing a tightly pent-up breath, and wrapped her arms back around herself. He was right about that at least. Anyone would be suspicious about why they'd married so suddenly, on the eve of her deportation. They would have to convince people the marriage was real, that they were in love.

Like they had at their wedding, she thought, the memory rushing back all at once. With everything that had happened afterward, she'd almost managed to forget.

The minister had been convinced, she remembered. And his clerk. They had thought it was real.

And so had she, she recalled faintly. Just for a moment.

Before she even realized what she was doing, she'd raised a hand and pressed her fingertips to her mouth, remembering.

Remembering just how real something pretend could seem.

Chapter Five

Luke stared into the darkness overhead, no closer to falling asleep than when he'd climbed into bed three hours earlier. He had too much running through his head, driving too much restless energy through his body.

Viktor. Solokov.

Karina.

He didn't let his thoughts linger on her, focusing on the question of Solokov and what they were going to do next. The man, or at least his minions, were growing more brazen. Not a good sign.

The most pressing matter had been dealt with. They'd bought her some time to remain in the country. Even if the marriage was challenged, there would be hearings and appeals that could last for months. Those would best be avoided, as forcing her to be at scheduled events would let her pursuers know where she would be and when. But they could worry about that as the situation arose.

And it would only be a problem if Solokov's men didn't

catch up with her before then. Which raised the issue of what they were going to do to keep her safe in the immediate future. Everything had happened so quickly today that he hadn't had time to beef up security on the house. That was the first order of business in the morning.

A morning that seemed so far away.

It was a far cry from his wedding night with Melanie. Unbidden, her face rose in his memory again. The way she'd looked on their wedding day. How beautiful she'd been. How happy she'd seemed.

Except before he even realized it, her face had melted into another. A face peering up at him not with joy, but nervousness.

Karina.

His wife.

And then it was her he remembered kissing. The softness of her lips. The tentative eagerness. The way she tasted. The way her mouth had looked afterward.

Swallowing a groan, he closed his eyes and took a deep breath, waiting until the memories, the sudden heat inside him, subsided.

Rolling over, he checked the clock sitting on the bedside table, seeking the familiar glowing red digits.

There was nothing there.

No, he realized, his eyes gradually spotting the dark shape in the darkness. The clock was still there. It just wasn't working.

There was only one explanation he could think of. The power had to be out.

The first stirrings of unease flickering in his gut, he

slowly rolled over onto his other side. The window on the exterior wall offered a view of his closest neighbor's house. Most of the windows were dark, unsurprising given the time of night, but there were enough lights visible to verify that the electricity there was fully functioning.

He'd experienced a few blackouts before and knew that if it was a problem at the power company, his neighbor's house would be affected as well as his. The fact that it wasn't meant whatever was happening was limited to his building.

The vague unease gave way to full-blown alarm, all of his senses immediately going on alert. He turned over one last time, searching out the open doorway to the room. He could see nothing beyond it but darkness. He stared deep into it, searching for any sign of movement, listening for the faintest trace of sound.

Nothing.

Nowhere close to being satisfied, he quickly climbed to his feet. His soles had barely touched the ground before he was making his way across the room, reaching for the gun he kept for protection and had left on his dresser. He probably should have kept it closer at hand, but he hadn't expected to need it. He still might not, but this was no time for taking chances.

The power had to be out for a reason, and given the circumstances, he wasn't going to take the chance of assuming a simple electrical short was responsible.

He didn't stop moving once the weapon was in his hands. He strode silently to the doorway, pausing just inside to listen again. Silence echoed down the corridor.

Slowly drawing a breath, he eased his head out into the hallway, his weapon primed.

Still nothing. Nothing moved. Nothing made a sound.

That didn't mean someone wasn't in the house.

He considered his options. If there was someone there, someone who was after Karina, that person wouldn't be alone. There'd be at least two, maybe three. Enough to take care of him and get to her. And if they had cut the power, not only would that make it easier to get past the security system, but it would also make it harder to see them in the dark. The possibility that it might make it more difficult for the intruders to see him didn't offer much comfort, especially because he didn't know what kind of equipment they might have. With the kind of deep pockets Solokov had, he could certainly afford to bankroll an operation that could purchase night vision goggles.

He could tell Karina to hide, but if anything happened to him, any intruders would have a clear path to her. Calling for help wasn't a possibility. Anybody who cut the power likely would have taken out the landline, as well, for good measure, and he'd left his cell downstairs in his office. A foolish move, but there was little he could do about it now. Even trying to get to his phone would be a waste of time. If something did happen, it would be too long before the cops managed to get here.

No, there was only one option available.

He had to try to get Karina out of the house and away from whoever might be inside.

When Luke didn't detect the telltale creak of someone on the stairs, he figured he had a couple of seconds to work with. He set the gun down just long enough to shove his legs in the pants he'd tossed over the arm of a nearby chair when he'd gotten undressed. He didn't bother with a shirt. The one he'd worn that day was in the hamper and he didn't have time to waste digging one out of the closet or a drawer.

With one last check to confirm the hall remained empty, he stepped out of the bedroom.

Moving on the balls of his feet, Luke quickly made his way to the guest bedroom he'd never had any use for before. When he'd bought the place, he'd hired a decorator to furnish it, not paying much attention to her plans, not really caring. Afterward it had seemed more trouble than it was worth to get rid of everything. Now it appeared she'd been right. He had found a use for the room after all.

Unsurprisingly, Karina had closed the door. He just had to hope she hadn't locked it. He couldn't risk the attention knocking would draw.

He eased his hand onto the knob, bracing himself to find it bolted.

Instead it turned easily in his hand. Exhaling silently, he edged the door open, not wanting it to make a sound that would draw the attention of any intruders. Making just enough room for himself to enter, he slipped through the gap, already beginning to push the door shut again behind him as soon as he was inside.

His eyes went to the bed. With the curtains drawn, the outline of her body was barely visible in the dark.

He didn't need time to adjust to the blackness to see her better. As soon as the door shut behind him, she bolted upright.

"It's me," he whispered before she could make a sound. "Luke," he added, realizing she might not recognize his voice, whether because of the hushed tones or brief time they'd known each other.

"What are you doing?" she asked, automatically matching the volume of her voice to his. Smart, he registered. She was smart enough to know he was being stealthy for a reason.

"The electricity is out."

He couldn't see her expression, but he sensed how she grew even tenser all the same. "You think someone is here?"

"I don't know, but I don't want to take the chance. Get dressed. We need to get out of here."

She obeyed immediately, getting to her feet.

"Did you call the police?" she murmured, the words barely audible.

"No time," he said.

She didn't argue or comment further, grabbing some clothes out of a bag sitting at the end of the bed and quickly pulling them over whatever she was already wearing. As she shoved her feet in her shoes, he opened his mouth to tell her not to bother taking anything with her. There was no need. She straightened and stepped up to him without reaching for anything else, leaving the bag where it was, clearly ready to go.

Smart, he thought again, feeling a reluctant trace of

respect. But perhaps not so surprising. After being in danger for more than a month, she'd no doubt developed some survival instincts if she hadn't already had them.

Without a word, he turned back to the door. He pressed his ear to it, not sure if he would be able to hear anything through the solid surface but not about to take the foolish risk of not trying.

Sensing nothing, he glanced back at her. "Stay close behind me."

He was about to pull the door open when she hooked one of her hands into the back of his waistband, perhaps taking his words too literally, perhaps just not wanting to lose him in the dark. The feel of her warm, soft fingers grazing the small of his back sent a jolt through him. He did his best to ignore it, along with the sudden pickup in his already-racing pulse.

She'd surprised him, that was all. Nothing more.

Easing the door open, he confirmed the hallway remained still and silent. Moving carefully, he stepped out of the room. She immediately fell into step behind him.

It hadn't taken long for the house to grow cooler with the power out and the heat off. It was more noticeable in the hallway than it had been in the guest bedroom. The cold air washed over his bare chest, and he had to try not to shiver. He knew he'd left a jacket hanging next to the back door. He'd have to grab it on their way out to the garage.

If they made it that far.

The stairs down to the first floor were only a few feet away. He felt her tremble, the shiver passing through her body right down to the fingers still grabbing the back of his pants.

When they reached the stairs, he slowly peered down them to the first floor. It was mostly dark, with only a bit of light from the windows down there.

And then he saw it. The flash of motion he'd been expecting, the one that shouldn't be there, shifting in the shadows at the bottom of the stairs. It was quickly followed by a narrow beam of light, piercing the darkness, briefly landing on different points in the room. Luke tried following the beam back to its source. In all likelihood, there was a hand guiding the light, belonging to one of the people who'd cut the power in the first place. If he could somehow use the light to gauge the person's location—

Then the light suddenly started upward in their direction. Whoever was down there must have located the stairs. He heard a low murmur. As he'd figured, whoever it was wasn't alone.

And now that they'd deduced he and Karina must be upstairs, they were on their way up.

He raised his weapon again, ready to shoot, even if he didn't have a chance in hell of knowing what he was aiming at. Even if he was only seconds away from being a much more conclusive target just as soon as that light landed on him.

He thought quickly, trying to decide if they should retreat, if he could tell Karina to go back into her room, if he should—

Suddenly the light was jerked upward, landing directly on him. He was so surprised that he was startled into freezing.

He knew immediately he'd made a mistake.

He tensed, bracing himself for the impact of a bullet.

At the same time, Karina gasped, the sound loud in the quiet.

The light jerked away from him, toward her, then suddenly went off.

And he knew they wouldn't shoot, at the same moment he realized why.

Because they'd seen her. She must have been peeking out from behind him.

Of course. Because their orders were to take her alive. It was too dark to get off a shot. They couldn't risk shooting, couldn't risk killing her and invoking Solokov's wrath.

Fortunately he had no such restrictions.

He aimed into the darkness at the bottom of the stairs, not caring whether he actually hit something. His sole purpose was to let them know he was armed and more than ready to use his weapon.

He fired.

Karina gasped again, and he realized she hadn't known what he was going to do. The sound was nearly drowned out by the echo of the gunshot, the noise loud in the close confines of his house. Almost immediately, he heard the muffled curses, the scramble of feet moving toward the back door. He cocked the weapon in his hand again, strictly for effect. To let them know he was ready to fire again.

He waited. Finally there was a muffled slam, the back door shutting, hopefully behind them.

Lowering his weapon without dropping it completely, he motioned forward with his shoulder. "Come on. We have to get out of here."

He quickly but cautiously led her down the stairs. There was always a chance that their intruders were toying with them by pretending to have left. Luke wasn't about to risk it. He stopped at the bottom of the stairs and peered around the corner down the hall to the kitchen and back door. The windows back there at least provided slightly more light than had been available upstairs. The corridor was still dark, but there was just enough for him to see that it was empty.

"Are they gone?" Karina whispered breathlessly.

"I think so. Let's go."

"Why? Don't you want to call the police now?" she said, still quiet but slightly louder this time.

"No," Luke said, starting forward down the hall. "I don't really feel like sitting around in the dark waiting for them to show up. We should get out of here, just in case they come back." He didn't think they would, but then, he didn't know what they were capable of, or what Solokov was paying. As long as the house remained demonstrably vulnerable to intruders, he didn't want her anywhere near here.

"Won't your neighbors call if they heard the gunshot?"

"Even if they heard it, I doubt a single gunshot at this time of night will draw too much attention. Anyone who heard it might think they imagined it."

They made it to the kitchen. He grabbed the jacket next to the door and quickly shrugged it on, forcing her to release the back of his pants. He immediately felt the loss of the heat from her hand and did his best to shrug off the feeling.

Tugging the door open, he carefully checked outside. Seeing no one, he moved out, pulling her with him, then reached back and shut the door. Even though he suspected the intruders were long gone, he didn't drop his guard as they made their way to the garage. Only when they were safely locked in the car did he allow himself to relax in the slightest.

Thirty seconds later they were tearing down the empty street away from his house. The nearest police station was in this direction. If someone had called them, they should have passed by Luke heading in the opposite direction. As he'd suspected, he didn't see a single cruiser. Once again, the police hadn't been notified. This time, he was automatically relieved, not needing to think about it.

"Where are we going?"

He glanced over at Karina. She stared straight ahead. In the brief flashes afforded by the streetlamps they passed under, she looked tired and drawn. He experienced a twinge of sympathy, immediately quashed. She needed to get some rest. They both did.

"We'll find somewhere to hole up for the night. Somewhere they won't be able to find us."

She simply nodded. After a moment, her mouth opened. She didn't say anything, releasing a deep, unsteady sigh that resounded in the car's closed interior.

The twinge came again, harder this time, deep in his chest. It took more effort to clamp down on the burst of sympathy this time, but he did it. Clasping the wheel tightly, he turned his attention back to the road.

His responsibility was to keep her safe, nothing more.

Chapter Six

The hotel suite Luke found for them was vast and luxurious. The main room alone was bigger than the living room in Luke's house. The doors at one end were open, revealing a bedroom containing a massive bed located prominently in the center of it. Definitely not the kind of bed intended for just one person, although it would certainly have only one occupant tonight.

"You can take the bed," Luke said, perhaps misreading her attention to it. "I'll take the couch out here."

Karina turned to find him standing a few feet away. Behind him was the door he'd paused to lock securely. Multiple bolts were thrown, the metal latch closed, preventing anyone from being able to open the door even if the locks were breached. The sight was instantly reassuring.

He began to pull off his jacket, revealing the T-shirt he'd purchased at a gas station on the way here. It was a size too small, the only one they'd had, the fabric straining against the dimensions of his body. She was too tired to even try not to notice.

He tossed the jacket over the back of a chair and turned back to her. "So what do we do now?" she asked.

He grimaced. "I don't know yet. But we should be fine here for the time being. Even if they track us down, it's unlikely they'll be able to make a move on us tonight. Breaking into a house is one thing. Breaking into a hotel full of people is another. Hell, we probably should have checked into a hotel from the beginning. It would have made sense and made it seem like we were really on our honeymoon."

Honeymoon. Of course. Because they were married. Her gaze was drawn once again to the ring on her finger. Married. Strange how she kept managing to forget that. But then it had not been very long yet. Less than a day. How many days would it take to begin to seem real?

She must have stood there, staring at the ring without saying anything for too long, because the next thing she knew he was moving closer, stopping just out of the range of her vision.

"Are you okay?"

The words were right, but the tone was as emotionless as ever. She lifted her head to find him watching her, his expression as cool as his voice.

She forced herself to nod, the motion unsteady. "It has been a long day. So much has happened. Viktor. Those men…" *The wedding,* she added silently, not wanting him to see how uncertain she still felt about their marriage.

"I know," he said. "But at least it's over. We're safe here for the time being."

"But we cannot stay here forever. And they will keep coming."

He didn't answer immediately, perhaps because he didn't want to admit what they both knew. "Yes," he said finally.

Again she wished he was the kind of man capable of comforting her, of offering a warm embrace or sympathetic shoulder.

And yet, as though brought about by her thoughts, he moved closer still, until they were only one step apart. "It's going to be okay. I have no intention of running and hiding for the rest of my life. I will figure a way out of this."

Of course he could say that. It had been only one day. He hadn't had weeks like she had to realize there was no way out of this. She couldn't even bring herself to pretend to agree with him.

Instead she could only peer up into his eyes, eyes it seemed as though she'd been searching for emotion since the moment she'd met him. And for an instant, she thought she saw something there.

Without thinking, she took that final step, closing the gap between them. Only after the movement was completed did she realize what she'd done. They were now face-to-face, their bodies almost pressed together. She should step back again. She knew it.

She didn't move. Her body didn't want to step back. It wanted to move even closer, drawn to the heat she could feel as palpably as if their bodies really were pressed tightly together.

Unable to do so, she waited for him to step back instead.

He didn't move, his body hard and tense, as he stared down into her eyes.

The longer she looked, the less his eyes seemed emotionless. Deep in those fathomless blue orbs, something flickered. Something dark and mysterious. Something that sent a sudden, unexpected thrill shuddering up her spine.

Again, she remembered what it had felt like when he'd kissed her at their wedding, the moment seared into her memory so strongly that there was no denying its reality. She wondered if it would feel like that again. His mouth was tantalizingly close. All she had to do was push up slightly on her toes, she thought, even as she sensed him beginning to slowly lower his head—

He suddenly stepped back, his expression hardening. "Don't."

Disconcerted, she blinked up at him in confusion. "What?"

"I realize that you've lost a great deal the past couple of months, and you must be feeling vulnerable. But don't get carried away in the emotions of what happened tonight. We have an arrangement, that's all. Nothing between us is real. Remember that."

"I remember," she said weakly.

"Good. Because I'm not looking for a wife. This is only temporary. You're pretty enough, but I'm not interested."

Her head snapped back, his words striking her speechless. Even if she had mistaken what she'd thought she'd seen in his eyes, what she'd felt between them, there was no reason to be so cruel.

Embarrassment burned through her. Was this her fate, to be humiliated by the men she married?

She longed to drop her head, to step back, too, to move away. Instead, something made her hold his gaze. And the longer she looked, she realized she'd been right. His eyes were no longer emotionless. An emotion burned in them, something she didn't immediately recognize. It wasn't the heat of attraction she'd thought she'd seen. It wasn't the contempt his words might indicate.

No, it was something else.

Anger.

She tried to make sense of it. Why would he be angry with her?

Unless he was not angry with her, but with himself, she thought as she stared into his eyes, now dark with something else. And there was only one reason she could imagine why he would be angry with himself.

Because she hadn't been mistaken. He'd felt it, too, the pull between them. He'd felt it and hadn't liked it for whatever reason.

And suddenly she was angry, too. He was correct. She'd endured a great deal the past few months. In the last twenty-four hours alone she'd been forced to marry a man she didn't even know to save her life, seen Viktor gunned down and barely escaped the intruders at the house. Under any circumstances, his behavior—laying the blame for whatever he was feeling at her feet—

would have been offensive. Having it come at the end of such a day made it even worse, one last cruelty she didn't have the tolerance to endure.

Without even thinking about what she was doing, she stepped forward and placed the palm of her hand on his crotch. He recoiled instantly, pulling his hips back and away from her touch. But not before she felt the evidence that confirmed her suspicion.

From the color that spiked in his face, he knew it as well as she did. She threw her head back and pinned him with a glare.

"I see you are as much of a liar as my first husband. So you have no reason to worry. I fell in love with one liar. I will not make the same mistake again."

She started to whirl away. He didn't let her, grabbing her arm and bringing her to a halt. She whipped her head back to face him in surprise, in outrage, even as the feel of his fingers sent a jolt through her.

He leaned close, his expression somehow even tighter. This time there was no mistaking the anger. "Don't kid yourself. I'm a man. I may not be able to control my body's natural reaction, but that doesn't mean I feel anything more for you than what any man would for an available woman."

"I am not 'available.'"

"That's not the signal you were sending out a minute ago." He slowly shook his head, a sardonic gleam in his eye. "Your husband's been dead less than two months and you're already making eyes at another man? That doesn't say much for you."

"I lost my husband a long time ago, and the last thing I want is a man."

He frowned, his eyes narrowing. "What do you mean you lost your husband a long time ago?"

"It doesn't matter. It would not interest you."

"Everything about your husband interests me. He's the reason all of us are in this situation, isn't he?"

She lowered her head, shrugging one shoulder helplessly. "I met Dmitri shortly after my mother died. My father died several years earlier, and I admit I was lonely. Dmitri was handsome and charming. He gave me so many gifts, wanted to see me every night. It was flattering, exciting. I had never known a man like him. He was so passionate about how he wanted to be with me forever. So we married. But then he began to change. He seemed to lose interest. It was then I learned what kind of man he truly was."

"What kind of man is that?"

"A man who is never happy with what he has. He grew bored easily, and he always wanted something more. From the moment he had a new car, he would look at other cars. When we moved into our house, he wanted a better house. He was never satisfied with anything he had, including me."

At first she'd wondered if everything he'd seemed to feel for her before their marriage had been a lie. Then she'd learned it was simply his way. He was like a child desperately wanting the shiny new toy, only to quickly grow bored once he had it. She had no doubt that he truly had been captivated before he had her, as he'd been with so many things. But once he did have her, the excitement had no longer been there for him, and he'd turned his attention to other things.

For a long moment, Luke said nothing. Then his fingers, still clamped on her arm, slowly loosened. He let his hand fall to his side. "I'm sorry."

He had regained his lack of emotion, and there was no way for her to tell if he meant it. It likely did not matter. "I had my work." Making beautiful homes for other people, trying to forget how empty her own was.

She bit her lip, remembering how she'd always wanted children. But there had been no pregnancies, as Dmitri had begun to drift away almost as soon as their marriage had started.

Now she was simply grateful she didn't have a child. This nightmare was enough of an ordeal for her. The idea of a child being pulled into it was too much to bear. Or would Dmitri have even done what he had if they'd had children and been more of a happy family? She would like to believe he would not, would have given more consideration to the danger it would place his child in than he had for her.

"Why didn't you divorce?" Luke asked.

"I think Dmitri liked having someone there to take care of him and do the things he couldn't be bothered with, even if he lost interest in me. And he was always concerned with money. That likely is not a surprise given what he did. He was also married before and had to give his first wife some money when they were divorced. I am certain he thought it was cheaper to stay married than risk losing some of his money to me."

"Why didn't you divorce *him?*"

She stared at him for a long moment, the answer so ridiculous she nearly couldn't give it voice, before an almost-hysterical laugh bubbled up from her throat. "Because I used to believe marriage vows were forever. That must sound stupid to the man I married knowing our vows would mean nothing."

He exhaled sharply, the sound almost a snort. "Not so stupid. I used to believe the same thing."

"Now I know better."

He shifted away from her, turning his attention to the window, allowing her to see his profile, hard as granite. "We both do. Nothing lasts forever."

"That is certainly true for us."

He nodded tersely. "So we're agreed. We keep this simple. There's no point letting things get too personal."

"Of course. That was the arrangement from the beginning." She couldn't keep the edge out of her voice as she said it, the implication that she wasn't the one who'd forgotten their arrangement.

If he caught the insinuation, he didn't respond to it. "Good."

He said nothing more, continuing to face the window, not looking at her. Karina had the feeling she'd been dismissed. A spark of anger lit in her belly. She quickly squelched it. There was no reason to be angry. As she'd told him, that would mean she cared, about this man, about his attitude.

Instead she forced a note of calm into her voice as she said, "I think I will try to sleep."

"Good idea. We could both probably use the rest. God knows what tomorrow will bring."

Tomorrow. She glanced toward the window, took in the city still cloaked in darkness. Morning was only hours away now. It seemed unlikely tomorrow could bring anything that could begin to compare with everything that had happened today, but as he'd said, there was no way to know.

She was tempted to simply walk away without another word. Instead she forced herself to offer a polite, slightly stiff, "Good night."

"Good night," he said without looking at her.

She quickly moved to the bedroom, firmly closing the door behind her. As soon as it was shut, she sagged against the solid surface and released a deep breath, trying to ease the tension clenching her insides.

Having the door between them did nothing to relieve the strange buzzing she felt beneath her skin. It rumbled through her, causing a tremor to shake her from head to toe.

Her anger had faded, leaving something else. The feel of him. She could still feel his closeness. Still remember the way he'd looked peering down at her just before she'd thought he would kiss her, his eyes dark with an emotion she now knew she hadn't imagined.

She gave her head a furious shake. What was she doing? She did not even like the man. He was too cold and contained, and, she now knew, a liar. He may have saved her life, but he'd never been even remotely kind to her in the process. She could be grateful for what he'd done, but she had no reason to respond to him so strongly and every reason not to. She knew that.

But her body did not seem to care what her mind knew so well.

And somehow, of all the things that had happened that day, that was the most disturbing of all.

Chapter Seven

After grabbing as much sleep as he could on the couch in the main room, Luke finally rose around mid-morning. He checked that it was a reasonable hour, then reached for the phone. He'd put off calling Viktor last night, not wanting to wake the man when he needed to be getting as much rest as possible to recover from what had happened yesterday. But he also didn't want Viktor to worry if he tried to reach them and didn't get a response.

His friend answered on the second ring. "Hello?" His voice was clear, bearing no trace of grogginess. He must have been up for a while. Luke wondered if he'd already attempted to call.

"It's Luke. I wanted to let you know we had to leave my place, just in case you tried to contact us there and no one answered."

"Is everything all right?"

"We had some unexpected visitors."

Viktor's voice sharpened. "Was anyone hurt? Karina?"

"No, we got away clean. We checked into a hotel for

the night. I can give you the number if it's not on your caller ID, but I don't know if we'll be staying here long."

"You probably shouldn't. And next time don't call from the hotel. It may be best if I don't know where you are."

Of course, Luke realized uneasily. Because if Karina's pursuers failed to locate her themselves, they would most likely try to track down someone who might know where she was. Viktor wouldn't give up the information willingly, but he still didn't want it at all in case they tried forcing it out of him.

"Is everything okay with you?"

"You mean beyond the bullet wound? Yes." Viktor sighed, the sound grim. "However, I do have news for you, as well."

Luke braced himself, wondering what could possibly have happened now and not at all sure he really wanted to know. "I'm guessing it's not good."

"Solokov is in the country."

Luke frowned. Now that was unexpected. "Where?"

"He arrived on a private jet a few hours ago and is holed up in a hotel in D.C."

"Why would he come here? He obviously has people here working for him. There's no reason for him to come all this way himself."

"It could be a coincidence. He might simply have business here unrelated to Karina."

"You don't believe that any more than I do."

A beat of silence echoed across the line. "No."

"For him to go to all this trouble, this must be personal to him."

"If it wasn't already, I suspect he will make it so."

"He must really believe she knows where the money is."

"Or else he simply has no other way to find it and has to pursue this lead to the bitter end."

It certainly made the most sense. And as long as that was the case, Karina would never be safe.

The memory of last night's escape came rushing to the forefront of his mind. The tension of those desperate moments. The sadness and weariness on Karina's face.

Anger tightened in a hard knot in his chest. "What's the name of his hotel?"

Viktor didn't answer immediately. "Why do you ask?" he said finally, a cautious note in his tone.

"I'd like to know where he is."

Another hesitation. "Are you thinking of doing something? Because the man is dangerous, and you're supposed to be keeping Karina safe."

"And knowing where the man who's after her is staying would be a good start, don't you agree?" When Viktor remained silent, he continued, "Are you going to give me the information or do I have to start making some calls? It shouldn't be too hard to find out on my own."

Heaving a great sigh, Viktor provided the name.

Although he was unlikely to forget, Luke reached for a pen and jotted down the information. "Thank you."

"Don't do anything foolish," Viktor warned.

"Stay safe," Luke replied. "I'll check in again later."

He disconnected the call before the other man could say another word.

He slowly replaced the phone on the table, already turning over a multitude of scenarios in his head. This changed things. It was one thing to deal with an unseen enemy thousands of miles away with seemingly limitless resources, who could simply send more people to do his dirty work if the previous ones failed or were foiled. It was another altogether to have that adversary in such close proximity, where he could possibly be dealt with in some way.

Solokov was here. Now Luke just had to figure out what to do about it.

"What's wrong?"

Luke turned to find Karina standing in the now-open doorway to the bedroom, her entrance having gone unnoticed during his conversation with Viktor. One glance and every thought racing through his mind evaporated in a flash.

She'd clearly just gotten out of bed, her hair still tousled from sleep. She was dressed only in a long T-shirt that reached mid-thigh, exposing her shapely legs. He tried to avoid looking at them. Unfortunately, there was far too much else to see. The shirt was thin, and she had enough curves to fill out what should have been a loose-fitting garment. The swells of her breasts, of her hips, were all visible.

Even pulling his gaze all the way up to her face didn't do much good. Her lush mouth was puckered slightly, uncertainly, making her lips look full and inviting. Her eyes were wide, and not even the haunted look in them could disguise the beauty of that particular shade of green.

She looked the way she had last night, almost innocently alluring, as if she had no idea the vibe she was giving off and just how desirable she was. He'd wanted to believe it was an act, that she knew exactly what she was doing, was trying to manipulate him. That seemed far less likely in the light of day. She could barely hide her anxiety, yet was still undeniably attractive, her appeal entirely natural and unforced.

Part of him hated her for it.

The rest hated himself for not quite being able to keep himself from responding.

She'd pegged him right. He was a liar, one who damn well needed to keep reminding himself that everything between them had to remain strictly impersonal.

"Luke?"

The sound of his name on her lips sent a charge through him. A tremulous note had entered her voice, and he suddenly realized how long he'd simply been staring at her, saying nothing. She probably thought whatever he'd been discussing on the phone was so terrible he was hesitating to tell her.

Better to have her believe that than know what he'd really been thinking.

He cleared his throat. "That was Viktor. Solokov arrived in the country this morning."

She blinked at him, her mouth falling open slightly. It appeared to take her a moment for all the implications of that statement to sink in, her eyes narrowing and shifting away in concentration, her mind no doubt running through all the possibilities as his had when Viktor had broken the news.

"He came for me," she finally whispered. "He must have heard about the marriage. He knows if he cannot force me to return to Russia and his men cannot capture me, he will have to come here if he wants to find his money."

It made the most sense with the timeline. It hardly seemed a coincidence that Solokov had suddenly left Russia for the United States within hours of their marriage, as he must have if he'd arrived earlier that morning. "It doesn't matter what he wants. He's not going to succeed."

She pulled her gaze back to his face, a dispirited gleam in it. "That is what Sergei told me. 'We will not let him win.' A few hours later he was dead."

Both her expression and her tone were so bleak that he felt something tug hard deep inside him. He did his best to suppress the feeling before it could gain traction. "He underestimated how much danger he himself was in. I won't make the same mistake."

"I heard you ask about a hotel. Was it where Solokov is staying?"

"Yes."

"Why did you want to know?"

He hadn't wanted to concern Viktor by confirming what his friend had already suspected, but there was little point in hiding it from her. She'd find out soon enough. "I think I want to meet him."

At first, she could only gape at him. "You want to meet him?" she echoed in disbelief. "Why?"

"I want to know what I'm up against."

"You don't know that already, after everything that has happened?"

"I learned a long time ago that nothing compares with looking an opponent in the eye and studying him or her in person. It's less about what people say than how they say it."

She raised her eyebrows. "I agree," she said, unable to keep an ironic twist from both her words and her lips.

It didn't escape him that she was referring to what had happened last night. He didn't allow the memory to surface, not about to let himself be distracted. "So you can see why I want to meet him."

"This is not one of your legal negotiations. The man is very dangerous."

"Believe me, I know that by now. I've also been thinking a great deal about how we can possibly end this. You can't hide forever. God knows I can't keep moving you all over the place trying to keep you out of his hands. Obviously keeping you in the country isn't going to be enough to stop him. If he's willing to come all this way, he's not going to give up anytime soon. The best, and perhaps only, way to put an end to this would be to convince him that you weren't involved in your husband's theft and don't know where the money is."

"I do not think he is going to be convinced."

"Not easily at any rate," he agreed. "Alternately, I can

make it clear that I have no intention of allowing anything to happen to you."

"You truly do not know how dangerous he is if you believe that will stop him."

"If you have any better ideas, I'm all ears."

She shook her head. "I do not. That does not mean this is a good idea."

"Well, it's the only one we have to work with."

"You think you can just go to his hotel room and he will let you walk out?"

"No. I'll only approach him in a public place where I know neither he nor anyone working for him can try anything. Knowing the hotel just means I know where to find him. I'll follow him for a while, see if he goes somewhere public where it will be safe to approach him."

"You say *you* will follow him. What about me?"

He thought quickly, considering his options. Obviously he couldn't bring her with him. Having her out and about in public would be too dangerous. They were better off with Solokov not having any idea where she was. "Maybe I can think of someone to leave you with for a short time."

"No," she said immediately. "I will not put anyone else in danger for me."

He didn't bother arguing, already dismissing the idea almost as soon as he'd given it voice. Anyone he trusted well enough to leave her with was someone who could be easily connected to him, and he really didn't want to endanger anyone else, either. "Then we'll find a hotel in D.C. and get you checked in. You can wait there until I get back."

Her eyes widened again. "Alone? What if they find me?"

"Even if they manage to track you down, you should be safe in a hotel," he said, confidence growing with every word. "For Solokov to come all this way, he has to want to deal with you himself, no doubt face-to-face. Anyone who comes after you will be trying to capture you to take you to him, not kill or hurt you. Even if they break into the room, which would be difficult as hell if we find one with the right security, they have to know there's no way to get you out of the hotel without a fuss. You can kick and scream and fight back, drawing the attention of other guests or hotel security."

Doubt was etched all across her face. He did his best to swallow his own misgivings about the plan. The idea of leaving her alone, all on her own, didn't entirely sit well with him, either, but he couldn't see any way around it.

He knew he should hire a security team and have her stashed away somewhere, surrounded by guards and alarms in some impenetrable location where no one could possibly get to her. And she couldn't get to him.

But he also knew he couldn't entrust her safety to anyone else. He might be able to get a recommendation for a reputable company, but anyone could be bought off as far as he was concerned. Regardless of how much money Karina's husband had taken from him, Solokov still had to have plenty left for suitable bribes. The idea of bringing anyone else into this situation seemed far more dangerous than leaving her alone, safely ensconced in a hotel where no one could get to her.

No. She was his to protect. *He* had to keep her safe.

"The alternative is to keep running, keep hiding," he told her. "Forever."

She lowered her eyes. "That is what I have expected from the moment I learned Dmitri was dead."

There was such a sad matter-of-factness to the statement he couldn't help but respond, no matter how much he didn't want to. He knew she meant every word. Her gaze was empty, her expression bleak.

The urge was there, the automatic instinct to take her in his arms and hold her, to draw her close until she wasn't so scared. His arms damn near opened of their own volition.

He managed to kill the impulse, pulling his arms tight to his sides.

Then, as he watched, a noticeable change came over her. Her posture stiffened, her expression going cold. She slowly raised her eyes, glowering at him for a moment, only then raising her head, as well.

"So while I wait, you will meet with him alone."

Besides the change in her attitude, there was an odd note in the question that made him uneasy. "That's the idea."

"What is the real reason you want to meet with him?"

"What do you mean?"

"Is it because you want to make a deal with him? Maybe you have had enough and are ready to be rid of me."

"You can't really believe that."

"It makes sense. I would not blame you. You could have been killed last night. You know what happened to Sergei, to Viktor. I'm sure you do not want to die, too. Solokov might even pay you to give me to him. You could make a profit. But you should know I will not wait helplessly while you sell me to him."

She raised her chin, her stare defiant, even if she couldn't quite hide the shadow of nervousness on her face.

"That's ridiculous," he told her. "After everything he's done, everything he's put all of us through, the last thing I would do is give him what he wants, for whatever reason."

She didn't say anything. She didn't have to. Her skepticism remained clear.

Luke sighed. "Look, I need you to trust me. We have enough to deal with here without me having to wonder if you're going to take off or something."

She grimaced. "The last time I trusted my husband he stole from a very dangerous man and caused all of this."

"I'm not…Dmitri." He stumbled on the final word. He'd been about to say "your husband," but of course, that's exactly what he was. That seemed to be the problem.

"I know," she said quietly, completely unconvincing.

"Do you? Because it doesn't seem like it. Unlike your first husband, I'm putting my neck on the line for you, and it would be nice if you could avoid comparing me to him."

"Maybe you are not so different."

"What do you mean by that?"

She cocked a brow. "You both have humiliated me."

This time there was no avoiding the memory of what had happened last night. He wasn't accustomed to feeling shame, had long ago grown used to feeling nothing, but he recognized the emotion that swept through him all the same.

He knew he'd been cruel, far more so than had likely been necessary. He'd needed to be, needed to push her away exactly as she'd suspected. Even now, he wanted to be angry with her. Needed to be angry with her. It would make things so much easier. Maybe not for her, but for him.

Except he couldn't be angry with her. Not now that he knew so much more about her relationship with her first husband, not when he could see the wounds the man had caused.

He could apologize for what had happened last night. It might help her feel better about him, ease the tensions between them.

He couldn't quite bring himself to do it. To do so would raise questions he couldn't begin to answer. He needed her confidence, that much was true. But he still needed to maintain some distance between them, as well, keeping things impersonal.

He could only look her straight in the eye and say, "I'm not going to betray you. Trust me."

She simply stared at him, her expression carefully composed, revealing nothing.

"Okay," she said finally, her tone as enigmatic as her face. "But I am going with you."

"No way," he said immediately. "It's too dangerous."

"I will not let you put yourself in danger while I hide like a coward."

"Cowards tend to have a higher survival rate than people who are too brave for their own good. That's what you want, isn't it? To live?"

"I also do not want anyone else to die for me."

"You want to protect me?"

"I want to help. All I have done ever since those men came to my house looking for Dmitri is hide. I want to do something. I can help you."

"How?"

He could practically see her mind turning. She raised her chin. "I can drive the car. I can wait there when you go meet Solokov."

He shook his head. "You would be even more of a sitting duck than if you were alone in a hotel."

"Not if I keep driving."

"What are you talking about?"

"If you approach him in public, his people will try to follow you. Do you think you will be able to return to your car and start it before they catch you? But if I am already in the car, you can get in and we can drive away before they can stop us."

As much as he wanted to reject any idea that involved her being out in public in plain sight, it made a certain amount of sense. "If you're driving around while I'm with Solokov, how will you know when to come back for me?"

He could see her thinking quickly. "If we buy two mobile phones, you can call me as soon as you are about to leave and I will know to come and get you."

And he wouldn't even have to say anything. Since he was the only one who would have the number, all he would have to do was place the call, and she would know what it meant from the fact that it was ringing. "Do you even have a driver's license?"

"Yes. I have my Russian driver's license and an international permit from when I made purchasing trips in Europe."

He couldn't help but be impressed. She'd come up with this plan on the fly and it seemed to make sense, certainly more so than leaving her alone and defenseless somewhere. A moving target would be harder to track down, certainly harder to catch.

He stared at her for a long moment, seeing her in a new light. She was still the same incredibly desirable woman she'd been five minutes ago. She was also more than that, her head held high, her gaze meeting his unwaveringly, as challenging as anything she'd said.

She was smart. He'd figured as much last night in her response to his sudden appearance in her bedroom, the way she'd responded to his instructions, not out of simple obedience, but because she seemed to understand what needed to be done. He'd just thought it was the kind of intelligence born of the survival instinct. This was more than that. She was smarter than he'd given her credit for.

Perhaps too smart.

He frowned as the suspicion took hold. A moment ago she'd worried that he planned to betray her to Solokov. Now she wanted him to leave her alone with a vehicle. The better to escape Solokov's men, or the better to leave him behind in case he was selling her out?

"How do I know you won't drive off and leave me behind?"

She quirked a brow. "You will have to trust me."

He didn't like hearing those words any more than he suspected she had. But there was no way around it. He couldn't think of a better solution, not for his safety, but hers.

And that was all that mattered.

Chapter Eight

The uniformed doorman in front of the hotel briefly rubbed his hands together, trying to warm himself from the early evening chill.

Sitting in the driver's seat of the rented car, Karina could see the white cloud that rose in front of his mouth, even from where they were parked down the street. She felt for him. It didn't matter that she'd turned the heater on for a brief time before shutting it off to conserve gasoline, so that it was warm in the vehicle. She still felt as cold inside as the man must, if not more.

"How long do you intend to wait?" she asked.

"Until he comes out," Luke said from the passenger seat. She sensed that, like her, he never took his eyes from the scene in front of them.

"That could be a long time."

"I know. Do you have somewhere else to be?"

Anywhere but here, she longed to snap. Instead, she held her tongue, pressing her lips into a thin line to keep her thoughts to herself.

They'd exchanged Luke's car for a rental before leaving Baltimore, arriving in Washington, D.C. in late afternoon. He'd already located the hotel, and they'd come straight here, parking in a spot that afforded a perfect view of the front entrance. They'd stopped on the way to the city to buy the two disposable phones for their plan, as well as clothes and some food, so they were prepared for a long wait. The bag lay untouched in the backseat, neither of them having much of an appetite.

It had been nearly an hour. Dusk had just begun to fall.

Solokov had not yet appeared.

She nearly asked how Luke could be certain Solokov would exit through the front door of the hotel. If she could persuade him there were many exits, he might see this as a waste of time.

Even as she thought it, she dismissed the idea. Luke would not be so easily discouraged. Besides, a man like Anton Solokov would not slink out through the garage or a back exit. He would walk right out the front and into a waiting car, no doubt. And after that they would follow him, to a public place, Luke hoped. Where he could surprise the man and force an unplanned encounter.

What would happen at that encounter, and what she should do while it happened, continued to weigh heavily on her mind, as it had since he'd first suggested this plan.

Karina fought the urge to look over at him, knowing there was no point. She could search his face for hours and she wouldn't find the answers she needed. And Solokov could appear at any moment, the possibility too likely to risk losing her focus for an instant.

She was reminded again of the words Luke had thrown at her yesterday. He didn't know her, had only trusted her because of Viktor. The same was true for him. She didn't know this man. The only reason she had to trust him was because Viktor did.

It seemed so little on which to risk her life. People were wrong about others all the time. She had thought Dmitri had loved her. Sergei had thought Solokov couldn't touch them. Who was to say Viktor wasn't wrong about this man, too? How well did he even know him?

She swallowed the lump that had formed in her throat and forced herself to speak. "How long have you known Viktor?"

"He didn't tell you?"

"He said you met at university."

"That's right."

Luke didn't elaborate, as though that were answer enough. And perhaps it was for the question she'd asked. She tried to think of a different approach to get the information she wanted.

"You must have been good friends back then."

He didn't say anything at first, letting the suffocating silence thicken to the point where she wondered if he was going to respond at all. "Yes," he said finally. "We were."

"And you kept in touch all these years?"

Again, he didn't answer immediately. If her attention hadn't been so firmly locked on the entrance of the hotel, she might have glanced at him. "Viktor did. He'd give me a call every few months to check in, see if I wanted to grab a drink if he was in town."

She frowned. It sounded as though Viktor had been a good friend to him, but Luke had not been much of one to Viktor. "So if he had not called, you would not have chosen to stay in contact with him?"

"I have a busy life, a career that occupies most of my time and attention. I don't have much extra time to socialize."

And yet, when it had come to their current situation, he'd had no trouble taking time off from that job. She suspected that meant his inability to find time for anything else under normal circumstances was entirely by choice.

"Not even with someone who was a good friend?"

"I'm afraid not," he said without the slightest trace of regret.

"Do you have many good friends now?" she asked before she could think about it.

"Like I said, I don't really have the time."

"That does not bother you?"

This time she did glance at him, at just the right moment, otherwise she might not have seen the slight tightening of his jawline. "No."

She expected the answer. That didn't mean she understood it, as familiar sensations washed over her at the very thought. The aching loneliness. The vast emptiness. The hollowness that came with knowing she was entirely on her own. She couldn't hold back a shudder. "I don't like the feeling," she admitted softly, almost to herself.

There was another of those long hesitations that made her think he wasn't going to say anything before he finally said, "You don't have any close friends?"

She'd once believed so. She'd spent years surrounding herself with people, as though to make up for the emptiness in her marriage and her home. But when she'd suddenly found herself in this situation, she'd been forced to think of who her true friends were, who she could turn to, who she could trust. And she realized she had no one she could trust with her life. Her employer at the design firm had been the closest thing she'd had to a true friend, and she likely had the connections to help her. But Anna's business relied on catering to the wealthy, many of whom were close to Solokov or would be wary of crossing him. When Karina had thought about whether Anna would risk her business to help her, she had realized she likely would not.

In the end, she'd had to turn to family, or at least the closest thing she had to it. Perhaps that was as it should be. Family was supposed to be there for you, regardless of the danger.

And in the end all she had done was put her family in danger.

"Not true friends. Not any who could help me with Solokov."

"I don't think many people have friends that good."

"Viktor had you."

He made a scoffing sound. "Is that what this is about? Trying to figure out why Viktor turned to me and whether you should trust me?"

She said nothing, unwilling to utter what they both knew would be a lie, not wanting to speak the truth.

"Viktor's word isn't good enough for you?"

"Truthfully, I don't know him well enough to trust his judgment. I had not seen Viktor in years, since he came to the United States to attend university. And of course, he stayed here afterward to work." Even with the strides made in the new Russia there had been more opportunities here. She knew Sergei had longed for his return, until he'd finally received the diplomatic appointment that allowed him to be close to his son.

"Unlike me, I'm sure Viktor's social calendar prevented him from making many trips back home," Luke said.

Karina didn't doubt it. From what Sergei had told her, with some regret, Viktor showed no signs he intended to settle down anytime soon. Even during the brief period she had stayed with him, Viktor had taken several calls from what she expected was at least one woman, perhaps the one he'd summoned to help him yesterday.

"Sergei wanted so much for Viktor to find the right woman and start a family."

"I'm not sure he ever will," Luke said. "Marriage never seemed to be his thing. I remember him asking why I wanted to get married so young, even though it sounded more like he didn't understand why I wanted to get married at all."

"How old were you?"

Another long silence. She sensed his regret at bringing up the subject. "Twenty-one."

Even younger than her when she'd married Dmitri. "So Viktor knew your wife?"

"He was a groomsman."

Something that would not have happened if they had

not been good friends. Luke would have asked Viktor to perform the duty. Viktor had agreed even though he thought Luke was getting married too young. Luke might have no room for friends in his life now, but he had at one point, good friends.

It was strange to think of them as friends. Viktor, who was friends with so many, and this man, who was so cool and unknowable. Viktor, who'd never settled on one woman for long, and this man, who she suspected still mourned his dead wife.

But as Viktor was friendly with everybody, it made sense that he would be friends with this man, as well. She simply didn't know whether she should be grateful for that fact, or whether she should be concerned that Viktor's broad standards for friendship didn't really mean she could believe his endorsement of this man's character.

But she did want to believe it, she thought as a fierce longing pulled at her. She did want to believe that this man wouldn't betray her, no matter how few reasons she had to believe in him, no matter how foolish it would be to do so. After all they'd already been through, with the way he still made her feel and she was doing her best to ignore, she wanted to believe her instincts weren't wrong and she could trust him. And deep down, she thought she could. Or was she simply fooling herself into thinking so?

Before she could come to any conclusion, Anton Solokov suddenly stepped out of the hotel and onto the sidewalk in front of them.

This was it, the entire reason they'd been sitting there

for more than an hour. She knew she should say something to Luke, or even just raise her hand and point.

Karina could only stare, the breath caught in her lungs, her heart hammering in her chest, her body painfully frozen. She hadn't doubted Luke when he'd told her Solokov was here. Knowing it didn't dilute the impact of seeing him in the flesh, knowing that he was here and so close. Every instinct made her want to duck low in her seat, to hide before he saw her, even though there was little chance of him doing so or trying something even if he did. He didn't so much as glance in their direction as he made his way to the car idling in front of the hotel, the back door held open for him by a large man in a dark suit. A bodyguard or one of his enforcers?

"There he is," Luke said, clearly not needing her help identifying Solokov. "Let's go."

Yes, that is what they would have to do now, she thought faintly. Follow. With numb fingers, she reached for the key still in the ignition and started the engine.

Without looking at him, she could sense Luke's growing excitement, the same anticipation she'd heard in his voice causing him to sit up straighter, his body tense with energy.

As did hers. Not with anticipation, though, but with dread.

This was what he'd waited for. Now he would get to do what he wanted to.

Now it was time for her to decide what she was going to do, too.

"ARE YOU CERTAIN YOU WANT to do this?"

A slight tremor shook Karina's voice. She didn't look at him, staring straight ahead through the windshield, her hands clenched tightly on the steering wheel.

Luke studied her, trying to swallow his own misgivings. He'd felt her tension growing all day. Karina had driven to allow her to get used to the car. It hadn't taken him long to see she was a good driver. He didn't have to worry about her getting pulled over while he was with Solokov.

Worrying about her taking off was something else altogether.

They'd followed Solokov from his hotel to the restaurant he'd just entered. Luke's intention was to give the man enough time to be seated before entering the restaurant himself.

Which was hopefully enough time to convince himself Karina wasn't going to bolt while he was inside.

"It's going to be fine," he told her, trying for his most reassuring tone.

"It is a waste of time," she replied. But there was no fight in the words; her tone was simply defeated.

"Maybe," he said agreeably. "But maybe it won't be."

She grimaced, saying nothing.

He unfastened his seat belt. "I'll call you when I'm leaving the table."

She nodded once, offering no reassurance she would be there when he emerged.

"See you then," he said, as much for himself as for her. And he climbed out of the car.

Closing the door behind him, he stepped onto the curb. He turned back to watch her drive away, hoping he wasn't making a mistake.

She pulled into traffic. Moments later, the rental car disappeared in the flow of brake lights.

Pushing his misgivings aside, he headed for the door of the restaurant.

Sure enough, Solokov was already at a table, his menu open before him. Two men, clearly bodyguards, were seated on either side of him, leaving a free chair across from Solokov. Perfect.

At his hotel, Luke had immediately recognized Solokov from the multitude of photographs of the man he'd found in his research. On the surface, the man didn't necessarily look like the ruthless figure Luke knew him to be. A tall, fit man in his late forties, he was well-dressed in a tailored suit that left no doubt to its cost. His mouth was curved slightly upward at the edges, making his expression seem vaguely amused. There was just a trace of arrogance in the way he held his head, his chin slightly lifted, as though he were looking down on the world. Luke knew his type well enough to be familiar with the look. It was the look of a man who was a success and knew it.

But there was an edge to the man the polished exterior couldn't quite disguise. His eyes were slightly narrowed, his gaze sharp as it swept over his surroundings. Luke braced himself for the man to make eye contact, but Solokov's attention didn't reach him.

"Can I help you?" the host asked.

"I'm meeting someone," Luke said without taking his eyes off Solokov's table. He nodded vaguely into the dining room, already striding past the man. He braced himself for the host to try to stop him, but naturally in an upscale place like this, the man wouldn't make a scene. Luke still felt the man's eyes on his back, no doubt waiting to see if intervention was necessary, as he wove his way through the tables to the one where Solokov sat.

He was a few feet away from the table when the bodyguard to Solokov's right noticed him. The man's eyes narrowed, his body tensing as though ready to make a move.

Luke stopped next to the open chair, setting his hand on its back. "Mr. Solokov."

The man slowly lifted his head. Luke saw the spark of recognition in his eyes. Solokov knew exactly who Luke was. At this point, he would have been surprised if he hadn't.

Still, all he said in response to the greeting was a laconic, "Yes?"

Luke could play the game just as well as he could. Without asking, he pulled out the chair and slid into it. "My name is Luke Hubbard," he said, keeping his voice lowered. "I believe you know my wife."

Solokov set down his menu and leaned back slightly in his chair. "Do I?" he said, sounding amused. "And who is your wife?"

"Karina Fedorova. Hubbard, now."

The man appeared to mull the name over before

nodding slowly. "Ah, yes. A charming woman. Recently widowed, I believe."

"That's right."

"And yet already remarried."

"When something is right, there is little point in waiting, is there?"

"Perhaps not," Solokov smiled indulgently. He reached for the glass of wine in front of him and brought it to his lips. "But with such a quick marriage, I wonder how well you know your wife."

"As well as I need to."

"How long have you known her? A few weeks perhaps? Not long at all."

"I know enough," Luke said without hesitation. "I know *her.* For instance, I know that she's been through a great deal lately. Her first husband was evidently involved in something…unsavory, and she's been put through hell because of it. Even though she had nothing to do with what he was doing, even though she knew nothing about it."

Solokov's eyes narrowed slightly, the only indication Luke's meaning had been understood. The amused smile never wavered as he sipped some wine and replaced the glass on the table. "Some might not believe that a wife would not have some idea of her husband's dealings."

"Men have been known to go out of their way to keep secrets from their wives."

"And wives from their husbands."

Luke didn't so much as blink as the man's implication hit home. There was something in the burning intensity of his eyes that made it clear that beneath the pleasant facade, Solokov meant every word. It wasn't conjecture. It wasn't the last-ditch hope of a man who had no other avenues to pursue if he wanted to retrieve his money. For whatever reason, Solokov truly believed Karina had been involved in Dmitri's larceny.

For just a moment, in the face of Solokov's certainty, Luke felt a hint of doubt. Despite the double meanings underlying the conversation, Solokov was indisputably right about one thing. Luke hadn't known Karina long at all. Perhaps didn't know her at all.

No. As soon as the thought entered his mind, he rejected it. He'd asked her to trust him. He had to do the same.

"I sense we have a great deal in common," Luke said.

Solokov's mouth curved farther, his amusement deepening. "Do we?"

"You strike me as a man who strongly defends what is his. So am I."

"A man must look after what is his," Solokov agreed. "Otherwise he is not much of a man."

A hard edge entered the final words, betraying an anger the man had been able to keep in check until then. And Luke understood.

Of course. This was about more than money. It was about Solokov's honor. He'd been stolen from, made a fool of by a man in his employ and perhaps that man's wife.

It was as he'd deduced that morning. This was personal.

He and Karina had each been correct in another regard, as well. Just as he'd said, looking into Solokov's eyes, he was able to take the true measure of his opponent better than he could in any other way.

And just as she'd said, this was a very dangerous man.

There had been no point in coming here other than to satisfy his own curiosity. This wasn't a man who could be convinced he was wrong or to do anything other than exactly what he wanted to do.

And what he wanted was to hurt Karina.

Luke felt his resolve harden. He wasn't about to let that happen. More than ever, he wasn't going to let this man get anywhere near her. He'd already wasted enough time with him.

Preparing to rise, Luke smoothed his hands down the front of his slacks, hitting the redial button on the phone in his pocket through the fabric.

"I should let you get back to your meal."

"And I'm sure you should get back to your wife."

Luke missed neither the veiled threat nor the little twist the man threw on the final word. The threat this man posed to Karina had been hanging heavily in the air from the first moment his eyes had met Luke's, but for the first time Luke felt a hint of fear.

Karina was out there alone.

He rose from his seat with a nod. He didn't offer his hand. Neither did Solokov. The other man looked away first, picking up his menu and turning his attention to it as casually as if he'd never been interrupted.

Luke had barely gone five steps when he sensed one of Solokov's men rising from his seat and beginning to follow. Or maybe both of them. Luke didn't glance back to confirm the suspicion, not about to reveal the slightest hint of concern to any of the men behind him. He kept his stride steady and unhurried as he made his way back through the maze of tables to the front, nodding to the host on his way to the door.

Pushing through it, he immediately turned his head to the left, searching for any signs of the rental car. He didn't have to look far. Almost as soon as his foot hit the sidewalk, the sedan emerged from traffic and began to pull up out front. The tension in his chest loosened slightly at the sight of her behind the wheel. Safe. At least one part of the plan had gone as intended. She was still safe.

He was already reaching for the door handle before she came to a complete stop. He heard the lock release the instant before he made contact. Opening the door, he quickly slid into the passenger seat. She didn't look at him as he did so, already glancing back over her shoulder to check the traffic. He barely had the door shut again before she was pulling back onto the street.

Luke reached for the button to reactivate the locks, only to have them slide home a split second before he hit it. She'd done it first, probably moving to do so before he'd even thought to. Smart.

He glanced back in the side mirror to see one of Solokov's men standing there, watching them drive away. From the man's intense focus on their retreating vehicle, Luke wondered if he was memorizing the license plate. They were going to have to change vehicles again. Not that they wouldn't have done that anyway.

When the man was finally out of view, Luke sagged back in his seat. He looked at Karina. She sat ramrod straight in her seat, her gaze steady on the road. "What happened?" she asked.

"He really believes you knew what Dmitri was up to."

He watched her reaction. There was none. "He said that?"

"In a way."

"So you did not convince him to leave us alone."

"No," he said slowly. "You were right. He's not a man who can be convinced."

He waited for a smirk or an I-told-you-so, some sign she was gloating.

She didn't move a muscle, simply staring straight ahead at the street before them.

He should have known better. She may have been right, but that was hardly good news. It meant she remained a target, that they both were still in danger.

"So what do we do now?" she asked.

"I don't know yet. Let's just drive." He glanced at the fuel gauge. They'd filled up as soon as they picked up the car, and still had more than half a tank. Even if Solokov's man had managed to get the license plate, there was little chance they could be tracked down anytime soon. They had time, and he needed it. Needed to figure out what to do next.

The evening hadn't been a complete waste. Now he knew exactly what he was up against. He remembered the thinly veiled anger that had slipped into the man's voice, the burning intensity in his eyes.

This was someone who would stop at nothing to get to Karina, and seemingly had the resources to make it happen.

Thinking about the odds that faced them, Luke experienced the first true hint of doubt that he might not be able to protect her.

Which meant he had to turn to the last possible person who could.

Chapter Nine

"I didn't think we'd ever get out of there."

Glancing from the empty street to the Don't Walk sign on the other side of the crosswalk, Luke grinned. "Don't look at me. Going to the party was your idea."

Her hand clasped tightly in his, Melanie chuckled, the sound of her laugh giving him that warm feeling he cherished in his chest. "Not one of my better ones, was it?"

"Nope," he agreed amiably. "We could have stayed home."

"You always want to stay home."

"Only if you're there. I like staying home with you."

Up ahead, the signal finally changed, giving them the clearance to walk. Luke automatically checked the street. It was still empty, traffic being predictably light this close to midnight. He started forward, Melanie falling into step beside him.

"I was at the party," she pointed out.

"Which is the only thing that made it tolerable."

She chuckled again. "For me, too."

The warmth in her voice sent another rush of emotion coursing through him, damn near sending a lump to his throat. That he could feel this way still amazed him after all this time. He'd seen the way his parents had looked at each other from the day they'd brought him home, but never thought it would happen for him. Never known anyone could mean as much to him.

But she did. He loved this woman. Couldn't remember what his life had been like without her. Couldn't imagine a future without her in it. She was his future. His life.

"I love you."

Though he'd been thinking it, she was the one who said it. He looked at her. She was smiling at him, the expression lighting up her entire face. Even if she hadn't spoken the words aloud, that look would have communicated the thought just as effectively. This woman loved him, just as much as he loved her, though it hardly seemed possible.

He didn't get the chance to return the sentiment. He never did, no matter how many times he had this dream, no matter how desperate he was to say it, knowing what was to come.

And he did know. What should have been a split second stretched on into an endless, suspended moment in time as what was happening suddenly merged with the knowledge that this was only a dream. He was experiencing it, living the memory, while simultaneously knowing it wasn't real. He was smiling stupidly at her, even as terror gripped his insides, clawing its way up his throat. He wanted to tell her he loved her. He wanted *to scream that she needed to run. He wanted to push her out of the way or do anything but stare stupidly into the love in her eyes.*

On cue, a light suddenly appeared behind her, a steady, insistent beam growing more intense, bearing down on them.

And the whole time, she kept smiling, not knowing what was about to happen the way he did, frozen in that look expressing the last emotion she would ever feel—

"No!"

It took him a moment to realize he'd shouted the word aloud. He must have. He wouldn't have been able to in the dream, because he hadn't said it then. Hadn't even known what was happening until it was too late.

Instead, the sound of it seemed to hang in the air, echoing endlessly in his ears. Other sensations gradually faded into his consciousness. His chest rising and falling heavily as his lungs desperately sucked in great gulps of air. The sweat pouring down his bare chest. The tension still gripping his insides. He stared blindly into the darkness surrounding him, until the faint outline of the room became visible. Another hotel room, one they'd checked into because he didn't feel like trying to find their ultimate destination in the dark.

Still his mind raced, his chest heaved. He tried to regain control of his emotions, tried to shake the memories, the images, still vivid in his head. He hadn't had the dream in years. It used to be a constant part of his nightly routine, a nightmare he relived over and over again. Along with others he didn't even want to think about. Eventually they'd faded, occurring every other night, then every third, until they stopped altogether.

Now, after years of peace, the nightmare, the memory, had come back to haunt him.

He didn't have to think hard to know the cause.

Karina.

"What is wrong?"

Her voice, coming so soon after the mere thought of her, sent a jolt through him. It seemed to float out of the darkness, almost ghostly and unreal, and he nearly wondered if he was still dreaming after all.

Then he realized her voice hadn't simply come from nowhere. It had come from his left, where the door to her adjacent room was. She must have opened it without him realizing it, the effects of the nightmare blocking out everything else.

"Luke?" she said again, softer now, this time with a tremor in her voice.

He was going to have to say something. He sucked in a breath, tried to keep his tone even. "Nothing. Go back to bed."

At first nothing happened. He waited for the sound of her door closing again, even as he suspected she wouldn't be so easily satisfied with that nonexplanation.

Then the light suddenly flared on. His head already turned in that direction, he saw her immediately. She stood in the open doorway, her hand on the switch. Her eyes, wide and alarmed, swept over the room several times. A pang of guilt pierced his embarrassment. If she'd heard him call out, she must have assumed something bad had happened, maybe even intruders managing to break into the room as they had his house. He must have scared the hell out of her.

Her searching gaze finally settled on him, her expression losing none of its fear. "I heard you yell."

He ducked his head and gave it a hard shake, scrambling for an explanation. Anything but the truth. "I... was rolling around and hit my hand against the headboard. It hurt like hell. That's all. Sorry to disturb you." *Now go away.*

Again, he waited for the sound of her retreat.

Again, it didn't come.

He finally lifted his head to face her.

She was staring at him, the fear gone from her expression. Instead, her gaze was steady and shrewd, her eyes narrowed slightly as she surveyed him.

"Do you want me to look at it?" she asked.

"What?"

She arched a brow, the gesture almost mocking. "Your hand."

Right. "No," he said roughly. "It's not that bad."

Her lips thinned, curving downward at the ends in a hint of a frown. Her eyes more than communicated her disapproval. She knew he was lying, and he knew that she knew.

No, it was more than disapproval, he thought. He had the feeling he'd disappointed her somehow.

Because he was lying. Because of what had happened earlier that night.

He'd asked her to trust him. Evidently she'd decided

to do so, because she hadn't left him. And now he was lying to her.

He had to. Anything but the truth.

"Why did you come back?" he said suddenly, voicing the question that had leapt to mind without thinking.

She frowned. "I heard you yell."

"Not into the room just now. Tonight. At the restaurant. What made you decide to come back instead of driving away in case I was making a deal with Solokov?"

She tilted her head. "You did not want me to?"

"You know I did. Are you saying that's why you did it? Because I wanted you to?"

"I could not leave you. I told you, I do not want anyone else to be hurt for me."

She was right, she had said that. But hearing her say the words was very different from having her back them up with her actions.

They weren't talking about just anyone being hurt. They were talking about him. She'd done it for him. She'd come back to save his life, even if it meant risking her own, even if it meant taking the chance that he'd betray her.

Yet she said it as though it were nothing, simply obvious.

Staring into the stoic expression on her face, knowing this woman had risked her life for his, he felt a strange flicker of emotion deep in his belly. It almost felt like—

A jolt of unease shot through him, warning him he didn't want to go there. He brushed the thought aside before it could fully form.

He supposed he should thank her. Except that he didn't want to. He didn't want to feel gratitude toward this woman, didn't want to feel anything for her. Certainly not that strange flicker that was far deeper and more disturbing than simple gratitude.

She would be an easy person to like, he thought with some reluctance. Smart. Brave. Loyal. She was a good person, one who didn't deserve the circumstances in which she found herself.

Of course, bad things happened all the time to people who didn't deserve them. He knew that as well as anyone.

But not to this woman. Nothing was going to happen to her.

"Get some sleep," he said roughly. "I want to get out of here early. We need to be on the road as soon as possible just in case they manage to track us down."

"You have not told me where we are going."

"Somewhere safe. You're going to need your rest. We have some things to take care of when we get there."

"What kind of things?"

"Things that will keep you safe," he said curtly. It was all that mattered. Any longer explanations could wait until the morning.

Because he remembered the last thing he'd dreamed, the image that had filled his mind just before he'd jolted awake.

In that final moment, Melanie's face had changed, until it wasn't her he was looking at, dreaming of, at all.

It had been Karina. Staring at him. Having no idea

of the danger barreling toward her. Not knowing she was about to die.

He didn't even want to think about what it meant. He only knew he wasn't going to let it happen.

No matter what it took.

Chapter Ten

Karina watched the countryside pass by outside the window and felt a strange kind of peacefulness fall over her. It may have been that the danger seemed less oppressive the farther they traveled from Washington, although leaving Russia hadn't had the same effect. Or perhaps the scenery was so beautiful she couldn't help but be affected by it.

And it truly was beautiful, bathed in the glow of the morning sunlight. They were in Virginia again, Luke had mentioned briefly when they entered the state. Not the same area where they'd been married, she recognized that much. They were away from any kind of city, traveling down country roads, some lined with thick trees, some open, revealing lovely flat lands.

When she'd left Moscow, she hadn't thought about where she was going, merely where she was getting away from. America was simply a place to hide. She'd never thought she would see much of it, never had any real interest in doing so.

But the experiences of the past few weeks had taken her much farther than she'd expected, from Washington to Baltimore to Virginia. She knew she'd seen only a small portion of this vast country. Russia was even bigger and there was so much she hadn't seen of it, either.

So many places she hadn't seen. So many she wanted to. So many things she wanted to do. Perhaps someday—

Something deep inside her recoiled. She did her best to kill the thought. There was no reason to dream, to make plans for a future when she didn't know if she would have one.

She didn't even know what lay in store for her in the next few hours. Luke had remained stubbornly close-mouthed about where they were going and what they would do once they arrived. She'd given up trying to get an explanation. Her questions had only gotten her a few vague responses that told her nothing.

She glanced over at him. He stared intently at the road in front of them, eyes narrowed, two little lines between his eyebrows. She could almost sense the tension simmering beneath the surface of his skin.

She had a feeling he wasn't trying to shut her out intentionally, which was the only thing that kept her from questioning him further. He seemed more distracted than anything, so focused on whatever it was he intended to do that he didn't have time to explain it to her.

She should have been annoyed with him. Strangely, she was not. Perhaps it was because she didn't think he was doing it to be rude or high-handed. Perhaps it was because she trusted that whatever he intended was the right thing.

She trusted him.

It was a strange thought. A day ago she hadn't even been certain she should. Maybe she still shouldn't. But she'd made her choice. Last night she'd had her opportunity. She could have left, could have escaped rather than risk his betrayal. Instead, she'd stayed.

When she'd received his call so quickly after leaving him, far too soon for any sort of deal to have been struck, she'd felt a massive amount of relief and known she'd made the right choice. A feeling that had only been heightened when she'd walked into his room last night.

She studied him out of the corner of her eye. The memory of the way he'd looked last night, stripped of his usual coldness and control, came back to her. He'd been sitting up in bed, his legs pulled up, elbows resting on his knees, with only the thin sheet draped across his waist. In those first moments after she turned on the light, before he could regain control, she'd seen a far different Luke Hubbard than she ever had before: wild-eyed, mouth agape, perspiration dotting his forehead and coating his bare chest. The raw, naked emotion on his face had struck her dumb at first.

He wasn't just a cold, unfeeling man. He was more than that.

A man who had nightmares.

It didn't matter that he'd tried to lie about it. She knew all the same. It made him more real somehow. He wasn't a man who felt nothing. Would such a man be so disturbed by a dream? No. Now she knew he was capable of feeling a great deal. And she couldn't help but look at him differently because of it.

Curiosity nagged at her, fierce and insistent. There was more to him than she'd first believed. A great deal more, she suspected. And she couldn't help but wonder what other mysteries lay beneath this man's cool surface.

Suddenly Luke was turning off the road onto a long driveway. She could see nothing immediately in front of her. Their destination must lay a distance off the main road.

"Where are we?"

"An old farm, nonworking these days. It belongs to a former colleague who's now living overseas. He's someone no one should be able to connect to me very quickly. It's his old family place and he's holding on to it because he's going to retire here someday, but there shouldn't be anyone here now. They shouldn't be able to find us here, at least not anytime soon. We won't stay long enough for that to happen. But it should be safe enough for a few days at least."

Almost as soon as he finished speaking, a two-story farmhouse sitting in the middle of flat fields came into view. A barn was visible behind it, as well as a fenced-off pasture. There was no one in sight, no animals visible. Obviously it was as he'd said. It was an old farm no one was working.

He pulled up in front of the house and shifted the car into Park. "Have you ever fired a gun?"

She jerked her head toward him, surprised by the question. "No."

He nodded once. "Then I'd say it's time you did."

THEY DID NOT HAVE ANY REAL luggage with them to carry into the house, only a few bags with more clothes and food they'd picked up along the way. Tucking his gun in the back of his waistband, Luke took most of them, leaving Karina to carry the few remaining ones and follow him. He stopped in front of the steps, setting down some of the bags and lifting one of the rocks lining the porch. When he straightened, there was a key in his hand.

"What if the key had not been there?" she asked curiously.

"We would have had to break a window."

Luke wasted little time once they made it inside. He dropped most of his bags on the floor inside the front door, keeping just one paper bag in his hand, and jerked his head toward a hallway in front of them. "Come on."

He led her into the kitchen, giving her no real opportunity to take in her surroundings. As far as she could tell, it was an old house, as the outside had indicated. It was quiet and still, a faint mustiness in the air, as though no one had been here for some time. The vague impressions were all she was able to absorb before they arrived in the kitchen.

Once there, he set the paper bag on the counter and began opening cabinets.

"What are you looking for?" she asked from the doorway.

The question had barely left her mouth when he began to pull tin cans from the cabinets, placing them on the counter beside the paper bag.

"Targets," he said. "For you to aim at."

"Why do you want me to learn to fire a gun?"

"Because you may need it to defend yourself some-day. I'm sure I don't need to remind you that there are some very bad men after you. You should have every resource possible available to you to stop them."

"Isn't that what you are for?"

"I might not always be around, like yesterday. As I said, you should have every resource."

She frowned as an uneasy feeling slid down her spine.

Having deposited more than a dozen cans on the counter, he glanced back. Catching sight of her expression, he returned the frown. "Do you have a problem with guns?"

She had never thought enough about them to care much. At the moment, thinking of facing Solokov or more of his men, it did seem better to have a gun than not. "No."

"Good." Scooping up a load of cans in one arm, he nodded toward the ones left on the counter. "Grab some of those, would you?" Without waiting for a response, he snatched up the paper bag in his other hand and made his way to the back door.

The request had been a question, but there was little doubt it had been an order. Watching him step outside without a glance back, she was nearly tempted not to obey. After a long hesitation, she picked up the remaining cans and moved to the door.

By the time she stepped outside after him, he was already a good distance away, striding toward a fence. She paused on the porch and scanned the area, that same strange peacefulness welling in her chest. It was beautiful here and quiet. The large red barn she'd noticed before, its color weathered from time and the elements, loomed in the background. Beside it was a pasture surrounded by the fence Luke was heading for. There was a chill in the air, evidence that it was not yet spring, but the late winter sun shone down upon the scene. It almost seemed to glow.

"You coming?"

The sound of his call drew her out of her thoughts. He was standing at the fence, the cans he'd carried now lined up in a row on the flat top railing. The metal glinted in the sunlight.

Karina made her way over to him. He took the cans from her and placed them in the row with the others. When he was done, he reached for the paper bag he'd brought, pulling out a box of bullets. Setting it on the fence, he opened it, then pulled the gun out of the back of his jeans.

When they'd stopped to buy the ammunition, she'd briefly wondered what it was for, finally concluding it was because he'd had to leave his house without any beyond what was already loaded in the gun. Now she could see he'd been planning this moment long before they arrived. She wondered why he had not said anything sooner. But then, most of the ride had been passed in silence, with neither of them saying much of anything at all.

"First let me show you how to load it," Luke said now.

He opened the weapon, and she watched silently as he went through the motions of placing the ammunition into it, explaining each step as he did so. She absorbed the words, but as she observed his movements, she mostly found herself staring at his hands. He had big hands, with long fingers and wide palms, but they moved quickly and deftly. They were a man's hands, beautifully formed, strong and capable.

Watching their motions, she could almost imagine them moving on her body with as much capability, sliding over skin, manipulating yielding flesh—

She swallowed hard, her mouth suddenly dry, and gave herself a little shake.

He began to reverse the process, unloading the weapon, closing it up again, then handed both it and the ammunition to her.

"Your turn," he said.

She hesitated just a second before taking them from him. The metal was cold, not even warmed from his having handled it so recently, and Karina felt a chill run through her. She'd never even touched a gun, nor had the desire to. She stared at it for a long moment, this thing that was capable of such destruction. Was it a gun like this that had killed Sergei?

Or could one like it have saved him? she reminded herself. Solokov's men would not hesitate to use such a thing. She could not afford to, either.

She did her best to replicate his actions, the whole time feeling clumsy and awkward.

But when she finished and looked up again, he appeared satisfied.

"Good. Do you think you can remember that?"

She nodded mutely.

"Then let's try some target practice."

He held out his hand for the gun. She placed it back in his open palm.

He started back toward the house, leaving her to follow once again. After making it about halfway there, he turned back, motioning for her to get behind him. Once she had, he raised the gun in both hands, aiming it at the row of cans now some distance away.

He was saying more, explaining his stance, how to hold the gun. Her eyes trailed down his body, taking in the firm lines, the way the jeans he'd purchased molded to the muscles of his legs and thighs.

She swallowed again, but this time she had a much harder time looking away.

She finally managed it, lifting her eyes just in time to see him take a shot, his arms jerking in the aftermath.

The distinct sound of something striking metal was immediately followed by one of the cans flying off the fence.

She couldn't hide her surprise, even if she did not know for certain why she was surprised at all. He would not be trying to teach her if he did not know how to use a gun himself.

"Do attorneys in America use guns very much?" she asked as he turned to face her.

His mouth shifted slightly in what might have been

a smile for him. "No more than any other private citizens, I suppose."

"So how did you learn to shoot?"

Immediately that faint trace of a smile vanished, his lips regaining their usual tightness. "I took lessons," he muttered. "Here, you try." He handed her the weapon.

Karina tried to match the stance he'd taken, raising the gun in front of her, both arms extended. She could tell immediately it didn't feel right. Her arms felt too stiff, her shoulders too tight.

"Here," he said, moving closer.

And then his arms were coming around her, his hands sliding under her elbows. A jolt passed through her as soon as their limbs touched. He hesitated in mid-motion, and she knew he'd felt it, too. She held her breath, waiting to see if he would pull away.

He didn't, putting his arms the rest of the way around her, sliding his hands down her arms and placing them over hers and the gun.

This time she felt a shudder quake through her body. His chest was against her back, the heat of his body searing through the layers of cloth between them. His head rested just above and to the right of hers as he leaned close, murmuring more instructions she couldn't even begin to process. Not with the low rumble of his voice vibrating through her body or the feel of his warm breath brushing her cheek.

It was all she could do to not close her eyes and sink into the sensations he was surrounding her in. Every instinct longed to ease back against the muscled hardness of his chest, to relax into his arms as though it were an embrace, to pretend it was. How long had it been since a man had simply held her? The man would have been Dmitri, of course, but it would have happened so long ago she couldn't begin to recall.

"Okay?"

The word managed to break through the fog of sensations clouding her mind. She nodded shakily. "Yes."

He pulled away, releasing her. She immediately felt the loss of his heat, his closeness.

"Go ahead," he said.

Nearly shaking her head to force herself to focus, Karina eyed the line of cans on the fence. She centered in on the one most directly within her aim. It seemed so far away, too much so for her to have any hope of hitting it.

But she would have to, she realized, resolve hardening in her belly. If Solokov came after her or Luke, she would need to do this. Nothing else would be as effective.

She narrowed her eyes, trying not to see it as a can, picturing the face of a man coming after her.

She thought of Sergei, dead in the street. She thought of Viktor, injured. She even thought of Dmitri, dead because of his own greed.

She thought of Luke. Hurt. Shot. Dying because of her.

She pictured Solokov's face, smiling, laughing despite the misery left in his wake.

Before she even knew she'd done it, she pulled the trigger.

It couldn't have been more than a second later, but it seemed like an eternity, as she tried to compensate for the recoil of the gun that rocked her body, her eyes barely able to remain steady on her target. She saw it all the same.

The can flew off the fence.

At first all she could do was stare in shock, her eyes going wide, at the fresh gap in the row of cans. Seconds ago there had been a can in that space. Now there wasn't. Because of her.

Triumph surging in her veins, she whipped her head toward Luke, surprise and excitement drawing an unfamiliar smile to her face.

He was still looking at the fence, his eyebrows slightly raised. The corners of his mouth started to tilt upward.

He finally looked at her, that pleased near-smile on his face. And then they simply stared at each other. Karina felt her joyous smile fade slightly, uncertainly, as she looked at him. His expression was neither as cold nor carefully blank as she was used to seeing. This was something else, something she'd never seen before. Something mysterious and unreadable. She didn't know what it was, but she felt herself respond to it nonetheless, the same way she'd responded to his closeness. Her heart, already pounding from the success of her shot, beat even faster. Her skin began to tingle.

The steady, mysterious way he looked at her might be unfamiliar, but the feeling was nothing new. She'd been this aware of him for some time. Since he'd kissed her at their wedding. Since she'd held on tight to the back of his pants as he led them through the house and she'd felt the heat of his skin against hers. Since they'd nearly kissed again in the hotel room in Baltimore, where not even her anger, nor his, had been able to destroy the strength of her attraction to him.

What was different was her own response to it. She no longer felt the need to fight it. It was only now, after last night, when she'd finally allowed herself to trust him, that it seemed acceptable to feel it. Feeling such things for a man she didn't know, didn't trust, was foolish. Feeling such things now...

Was no less foolish, of course.

He made that clear as he lowered his eyes with a sharp nod, whatever she'd thought she'd seen on his face quickly draining away.

"Good job," he said roughly. "Let's do some more to make sure it wasn't just beginner's luck."

He returned his attention to the line of cans, seemingly waiting for her to regain her stance and take another shot.

She did the same, lifting the gun and choosing a new target. She tried her best to calm her racing heart and focus on the shot alone.

Something may have changed in the way she viewed him, but it did not change how things were between them. He was not truly her husband, not in any way that mattered. It was as he had said. Better not to let things get too personal.

There was no point.

Chapter Eleven

Luke stood in the center of the living room, at a complete loss what to do next. Ever since last night, his actions had been fueled by the plans he'd formulated. They would come here. He would teach her to shoot. She would be better able to protect herself should the occasion arise. And they had done that. Now his plans had been exhausted, with no new ones coming to mind. They were safe for the time being, at least enough so that the need to run had slightly abated for the moment. He'd had the completed forms they needed to file with Immigration sent to his assistant yesterday for her to handle. There was nothing he needed to be doing in the immediate future. He wished there was. He needed something to think about, something to distract him from the ideas, the images, racing through his head.

Karina had disappeared somewhere in the house. Maybe the bathroom. Maybe the bedroom to rest. She'd said something before she'd left, words he'd barely heard and hadn't registered, his thoughts elsewhere, as they were now.

He stared blankly in front of him, not seeing anything in his range of vision.

He saw only her.

The memory of Karina's smile remained at the forefront of his mind, unwavering, blocking out everything else. The way she'd looked when she'd taken that first shot and the can had flown off the fence. It hardly mattered that it had proven to be a lucky shot and she'd missed her next two. The only thing that mattered was that she'd made that one and suddenly looked back at him, the biggest smile imaginable stretched across her face, her eyes aglow with pleasure and surprise.

He'd seen her fear. He'd seen her anger.

He'd never seen her joy.

Even now, just remembering it, he felt the echo of its impact seize his chest again. His pulse had already kicked into a higher gear in response to the shock, the thrill of her unexpected success. Her smile had caused the fast cadence to stutter unevenly. He'd almost stopped breathing, or maybe he had. Maybe that had been the cause of the tightness in his chest when all he could do was stare back helplessly.

He'd almost forgotten what that was like, to have a woman smile at him like that, to bask in her pure joy, and be helpless to do anything but smile back.

And he almost had, until he'd managed to regain control and kill the instinctive reaction, even if he hadn't managed to completely kill the feeling deep inside that caused the impulse. Even now, just at the memory of it, some small part of him wanted to smile.

Instead he frowned, blinking furiously as if that would have the slightest impact on clearing his mind's eye. He pulled out his phone. He'd put off calling Viktor as long as possible, knowing this was a conversation he didn't want to have. Suddenly it seemed far less painful than standing there stewing in his present thoughts.

Viktor picked up almost immediately. "Hello?"

"It's Luke."

"Thank God. I was getting worried. Is everything okay?"

"Fine. We moved locations again, somewhere safe for the time being. Solokov shouldn't be able to find us here."

"Good. Now what's wrong?"

"Who said anything's wrong?"

"I've known you long enough to be able to tell. Now what is it?"

Luke crossed to the liquor cabinet on the opposite wall. This was a conversation that definitely called for a stiff drink. "I've been thinking about this situation we're in and how we're going to get out of it."

"Any ideas?"

He set a shot glass on the counter and reached for a bottle of vodka. It seemed particularly fitting, given the circumstances. "I wish I had one. I can't keep shuttling her from location to location until Solokov gives up, especially since I don't think he's going to."

"I told you that before, when I brought Karina to you, did I not?"

"Yeah, well, now I've seen it for myself."

A dangerous silence echoed across the line. "What do you mean?"

Luke took a breath and finished pouring the drink. No turning back now. "I went to see him."

Viktor's explosion was instantaneous. "Damn it! I knew you were going to do something foolish."

"Then congratulations on being right." He raised the glass and drained it in one swallow.

"You think this is a joke? He could have killed you."

"I approached him in a restaurant in a room full of people. He couldn't have done anything there."

"You don't know that. You don't know him. And he didn't have to do anything there. He could have had someone follow you. Someone could have trailed you to where you are now."

"No one did. Believe me, I was careful."

"And where was Karina when you met Solokov?"

Luke hesitated, knowing the reaction he'd get, before answering. "In the car."

There was a momentary pause, as though Viktor didn't believe what he'd just heard and required a moment to comprehend it. "You left her alone?" Rather than the outrage or shock Luke might have expected, every word simmered with barely contained anger.

He instinctively wanted to offer some kind of justification, but he knew there was none he could give. It had been a foolish decision he was damn lucky hadn't gone very badly. "Yes."

"What were you thinking?" This time Viktor didn't bother to hold back his rage.

"I was thinking there had to be a way to get out of this situation before anyone else is hurt, and the only one available was to try to talk some sense into the man and convince him Karina doesn't have what he wants."

"The man flew halfway around the world to deal with her personally. Did you really think you could convince him to turn back without his money?"

"I had to try."

"And did it work?"

"No."

"What did he have to say?"

"Nothing blatant. Just a lot of innuendo that made it clear he didn't believe me when I said Karina wasn't involved in her husband's misdeeds."

"So you put Karina's life at risk for nothing."

Yes. He reached for the bottle of vodka again. "Not for nothing. For a chance to save it."

"Bull," Viktor shot back. "You didn't do it for Karina at all. It was about Melanie, wasn't it?"

Everything in Luke went very still. His hand froze, fingers centimeters from the bottle. "If it is, then it has been from the beginning. That's why you brought Karina to me, isn't it? Because of Melanie?"

Viktor didn't answer immediately, the first indication he may have realized he'd gone too far.

When he did speak, his tone was calmer, a cautious note in his words. "If you're asking if I suspected that what happened to Melanie would convince you to help

Karina, then no. If anything I thought it would make it less likely."

"Bull." Luke tossed Viktor's previous comment back at him. Every bit of anger he'd wanted to throw at the man since the moment Viktor had appeared on his doorstep with Karina and made his request surged to the surface. He dropped his hand, no longer needing the drink, too furious to even contemplate it. "You knew exactly what you were doing."

"It's true. I did think what happened to Melanie would make you more determined to keep her safe if you agreed. At the same time I had my doubts you would agree for the same reason."

"So that was what the veiled reference to my parents was for? The 'losing family' schtick?"

"I did what I had to do," Viktor said without the slightest trace of regret.

"You bastard. You knew how I felt about Melanie—"

"Of course I know. I introduced you, remember?"

"—and you know what I went through when my parents died, and you didn't give a damn about it as long as you got what you wanted."

"Karina's life is in danger, and yes, that was more important to me than the misery you've been stewing in for all these years."

"Don't count on me ever forgiving you for this."

"I'm not asking for your forgiveness. I apologize for nothing."

"Yeah, well, don't ask me for anything else, either. Especially any favors."

Too furious to spend another second talking to the man, Luke disconnected the call and slammed the phone down. He braced his hands on the counter and stood there, seething, shaking from it. He'd known all along what Viktor was doing. He'd told Karina as much after their wedding. Had that really been only two days ago? But hearing the man confirm it, and do so unrepentantly, without the slightest concern for the turmoil he'd known it would cause, somehow made it even worse.

"What happened to your wife?"

Karina's softly spoken question seemed to come out of nowhere. Luke started, turning to find her standing in the doorway, her entrance unnoticed in the heat of his conversation with Viktor. She stood with her arms folded over her chest, her back straight. It was clear she'd been there for some time, no doubt long enough to have heard plenty of the conversation. He hadn't given enough thought to his location when he'd made the call, not really expecting the conversation to travel to the places it had, to reveal anything more than she already knew. Another mistake. He should have considered the likelihood she would wander into the main room directly in the center of the house at some point during the call. Even if she hadn't, she likely would have been drawn by the sound of his raised voice.

The silence stretched on, but she didn't repeat the question. She simply stared at him and let it hang there in the air, her expression resolute.

He was tempted to tell her it was none of her business, which it wasn't, or simply not answer at all.

From the look on her face, she wouldn't let him get by with either response. He'd spent enough time with her by now to know she wasn't the type of person to back down from a challenge. If he was completely honest, he respected that about her. She was tough, more so than he would have expected when they first met. At the moment, though, he'd like it a hell of a lot more if she were the type of person who would go away and leave him alone.

He turned away from her, reaching for the bottle of vodka again. "She died."

"How?"

He poured slowly, taking his time with both the liquor and the answer. "Car accident."

"And Viktor believed that was why you would agree to help me? Because you would not let another woman die, another wife?"

His mouth curled in a contemptuous sneer. "You'd have to ask Viktor about that."

Karina swallowed her rising impatience in the face of his short, unrevealing answers. She doubted losing her temper would cause him to give her the information she wanted, needed. And she did need it, needed to understand this man who remained such a mystery to her despite everything that had happened and all the time they'd spent together in the past few days. "Tell me about the car accident. What happened?"

He didn't say anything for a long moment. He set the bottle next to the glass and stared at them both without touching either. As she had before, she wondered if he was going to answer at all. But also as before, she was prepared to wait. Her heart was pounding furiously in her chest, her desperation for the truth that pressing.

"We were walking home after a party. We were in the middle of the crosswalk when a car plowed through the intersection and hit us. I survived. Melanie didn't."

He said it so plainly, dispassionately, as though relating something that had happened to people he didn't know and certainly didn't care about. Karina wasn't as unaffected. Though she didn't know what his wife had looked like, she could picture the scene clearly. The image drove a lump into her throat.

"Were you hurt?" she managed to ask.

"Not enough to matter. Melanie died at the scene."

"Did they catch the driver?"

"No. They never did."

"Is that why you wanted to meet Solokov? To confront him the way you could not confront the person who killed your wife?"

"You sound like Viktor."

"That is not an answer."

Silence. "I don't know."

Karina carefully examined the words for any trace of deception. She found none. If that had been the reason, and she suspected it was, the urge had been a subconscious one, not something he'd done with that express purpose in mind.

"And your parents? How could Viktor use them against you?"

"The Hubbards weren't my biological parents. I was adopted as a child, after my birth parents died. Viktor knew his comments about blood not being a requirement for family would have particular resonance with me."

"And they died, too?"

"They were killed in a home invasion two months after Melanie's death. Someone broke in, evidently to rob them, and ended up killing them. They'd barely gotten back home after the funeral and they were dead, too."

The words were spoken as emotionlessly as ever, with no trace that the subject affected him in the least. That didn't stop them from affecting her. Sadness welled inside her. So much loss. And she had thought she'd lost so much. If only she'd known.

"Do you have any other family?"

Again, he didn't answer right away, staring blankly at the liquor cabinet before him. Finally, he said, "No."

She narrowed her eyes. "You are lying again."

He sighed heavily, then shrugged. "I used to have brothers."

"Brothers?" she echoed. "More than one?"

His mouth tightened before he answered. "Four."

"Where are they?"

"I have no idea. We were separated after our parents died."

His first parents, she discerned with a pang. Adult children wouldn't have been separated. "How old were you?"

"Five. I was the youngest," he added almost as an afterthought.

So young. "You never saw your brothers again?"

"I heard from one of them a few years ago. He wanted to meet. I told him I wasn't interested."

"Why not?"

"What's the point? I don't even remember them. I don't have room in my life for a bunch of long-lost siblings I don't even know."

No, he wouldn't, she thought, sorrow heavy in her chest. He'd lost too much already. Two sets of parents, a beloved wife.

He glanced at her, impatience flashing across his hardened face once he took in hers. "Don't."

She frowned, not understanding. "Don't?"

"Don't feel sad for me," he said. "If anything you should be worried for yourself."

"Why?"

"You were worried about getting me killed. You should have worried about entrusting your life to a stranger, especially when people who get close to him have an unfortunate tendency to die."

Except she had worried about that, she thought dully. Wondered about the wisdom of placing her fate in a stranger's hands. She just hadn't known about the rest.

And now that she did… Part of her recoiled at his words, instantly rejecting them. She wanted to believe this was nothing more than another attempt to push her away, but it was painfully clear that he believed exactly what he was saying. His words contained none of the carefully emotionless calm nor the spark of anger that showed how much he was trying not to feel anything at all. There was only a trace of bitterness and a grim frankness.

What was it? Was he afraid of getting close to anyone again, afraid of enduring the pain of losing someone else? Or did he simply have nothing left to give?

She peered into his eyes, searching for the answers. There were none there, of course. There was nothing.

And suddenly she was angry. The fury surged within her, hot and fierce. "You are wasting your life."

For just a second, his eyes widened slightly in surprise. "What are you talking about?"

"You are all alone when you don't need to be. You have brothers you don't talk to. You have friends who clearly still care about you, people you can turn to. But you choose to be alone. Do you really think your parents, your wife, would want you to live this way? Alone? Having no one?"

"They're dead," he said coldly. "Their opinions are no longer relevant."

"I think they would be very sad."

"Your opinion was *never* relevant. There's nothing personal between us, remember?"

Liar, she thought, longing to spit the word at him. The desire was minor compared to everything else she was feeling.

"At our first meeting I told you I did not want to die. But it is more than that. I want to live. They may sound like the same things, but they are not. Every day since Dmitri's death I have faced the possibility that I might die at any moment."

"Nothing's going to happen to you."

"Are you the only one who is allowed to think you might die? That is what today was about, was it not? Teaching me to shoot a gun? Because we both know you intend to protect me as long as you are able. The only reason to teach me to protect myself is in case there is a time you cannot."

He said nothing, his silence agreement enough.

"I am not a child. I know what might happen, the way this most likely will end. I will be hiding and running for as long as I can, perhaps for the rest of my life or at least Solokov's. He had Sergei murdered, came all the way to this country to get what he wants. He is not going to give up. And if he finds me, he will want to know where the money is, something I cannot tell him. So he or his men will do whatever they can to force me to tell them something I cannot. And in the end, they will kill me."

"That's not going to happen," he said fiercely.

She ignored him. "I know all of this, and I have spent many hours thinking about my life, about all the years I wasted with a man who did not love me, all the years I spent being unhappy. Because I thought I had no choice and that is how it had to be. But you have a choice, and you choose to be alone."

"It's none of your business. You're not really my wife. You need to remember that."

"One day it will be too late. You can pretend your brothers mean nothing to you. You can pretend you do not care. But if something happens to one of them, it will not matter that you did not talk to him or spend time with him. You still will have lost him forever. And then you will never be able to—"

He slammed his closed fist on the countertop, the action so abrupt, so unexpected, she was startled into silence. She watched the broad line of his shoulders shudder slightly. He released a ragged breath, the sound loud in the sudden quiet of the room.

"I...*can't.*"

The word was rough, raw, as though pulled painfully from someplace deep inside him. There was none of the carefully maintained coolness hiding his true feelings. And she knew it was the most honest thing he had ever said to her.

A hard lump formed in her throat. She could only stare at him, her anger forgotten, replaced with sorrow.

"Then I have to feel sad for you," she said softly.

He gave no outward reaction, and suddenly she could no longer bear to look at him. Her heart aching painfully in her chest, she turned and walked quickly from the room.

LUKE LISTENED TO THE SOUND of her footsteps retreating. He tried to draw in a deep breath and calm his racing heart. His throat was too constricted, his chest too tight, and the air caught as it entered his lungs, making it feel like he was choking.

Damn it. He eyed the bottle on the counter, then shoved it away, knowing it wouldn't do any good.

She'd finally managed to do what she'd nearly done numerous times over the past several days, caused him to lose his firm grip on his control, forced him to reveal things he'd never wanted to admit, made him feel things he didn't want to. Even though she was gone, they continued to flood his head—images he didn't want to remember, things he didn't want to feel—as though she'd torn down a breach wall with her words alone. It would take a great deal of effort and energy to rebuild that wall, but by God, he would do it.

Because he couldn't live like this, couldn't deal with the strange longing that struck him at the thought of his brothers, faces he barely remembered but wished he could. Couldn't handle the memory of seeing Melanie right after the accident and knowing even before he reached out to touch her or said a single word that she was dead.

Couldn't take the idea of anything happening to Karina and knowing he'd lost one more person.

Despite his protests to the contrary, he was as realistic about the situation as she was. He knew the odds of keeping her away from Solokov indefinitely. He couldn't protect her alone, and trusted too few people to believe anyone couldn't be gotten to, or sacrificed in Solokov's quest to avenge Dmitri's theft. Sooner or later there would have to be a reckoning. And he was aware what the final result would most likely be.

Even the thought of it sent agony shafting through him. He could imagine it too well. Karina, dead, eyes closed forever, blood streaked across her face, dripping into her hair. Like Melanie, although what would be done to Karina would be far different.

Viktor had been right about one thing. He had been determined to keep Karina safe, had no intention of letting anything happen to her. But he'd also vowed not to care about her, not to let himself get too close. A vow he'd failed to uphold, at his own peril.

Because losing Melanie hadn't killed him, no matter how much it had felt like it would at the time. Neither had losing his parents.

But he knew without the slightest doubt that losing this woman would finally be the end of him.

Chapter Twelve

Another strange bedroom, another sleepless night.

Karina shifted uneasily on the bed, unable to find a comfortable position on the mattress. She knew it had more to do with her than the bed.

Images kept flickering through her mind. Remembered sensations crawled along her skin, reminding her. The way his fingers had looked when he'd loaded the gun. How his body had felt pressed to hers. The heat of his breath washing against her hair, her cheek.

Things had been tense between them ever since their confrontation that morning. He'd barely looked at her, had hardly said two words to her, the rest of the day. They'd each kept their distance until dinner, which had been a silent affair.

By then, her anger and frustration and sorrow had faded. What remained was what she felt now, the memory of that closeness, which only seemed more intense in the wake of their conversation. Now that she finally understood him, now that she'd gotten a sense of who he really was, it only heightened her reaction to him.

She'd watched him at dinner, and though she would bet anything he would deny it, she'd sensed him watching her, too. And she'd known. He still wanted her, as much as he had in that hotel room two nights ago, as much as she wanted him. The tension, far different from anger or animosity, seemed to hang in the air between them. In the end, he'd practically bolted from the room to escape it.

She'd never been so aware of a man, not even Dmitri. She'd been so young when she'd met him. He'd made her feel things, of course, but even those initial stirrings had carried with them a sense of sweetness, of innocence, as she'd felt things unlike anything she had before.

There was nothing innocent about how Luke Hubbard made her feel. She was no longer young. She was a woman now, one who had experienced what she'd believed was love and what it was to lose it. And what she felt for him were the desires of a woman, more fierce and insistent than anything she'd ever known.

Desires that would most likely go unfulfilled, one last disappointment, something she'd wanted and had to accept she would never have.

Even as she thought it, her mind rebelled against it. She didn't accept it. Didn't accept that she had to take this disappointment like all the other missed chances.

She didn't know what the morning would bring. She didn't know what could happen an hour from now, or even a minute. She only had this moment, right now.

And she was wasting it lying in bed, thinking about a man who was in the next room.

A man she wanted to touch. A man she wished would wrap his arms around her once more.

If she wanted that, she needed to do it now. There may not be another chance.

And she did want it.

He may not want to live, but she did.

She didn't allow herself to waste another thought, another second. Thrusting the covers aside, she rose from the bed and strode from the room.

His door was open, perhaps as a precaution in case anything should happen in the night. She could see Luke stretched out on the bed, a thin sheet covering him, his chest bare. He stirred as soon as she stepped into the doorway. Or perhaps he was as restless as she'd been and would have been moving whether or not she entered. Either way, she had barely placed one foot in the room, the motion not even making a sound, when he rolled over on the bed toward her, then suddenly sat up, much as she had when it was he who'd entered her room.

"What's wrong?" he demanded, his voice devoid of any trace of sleep. Even as the words left his mouth, he was reaching for the gun sitting on the table beside the bed.

"Nothing," she said, moving closer. She grabbed the bottom of her shirt and pulled it over her head. Cool air washed over her skin. She barely felt it, too much heat flooding her body for the chill to make an impact.

He froze, his hand poised halfway above the table. The shadows concealed his face and she couldn't see his expression in the darkness. She could still feel his eyes pinned on her. The warmth of his gaze washed over her, trailing down from her face to her breasts.

"What are you doing?" he said. A gratifying thickness marred the usual calm of his voice.

She tossed the shirt aside. Her underwear followed moments later. "Living."

She'd stepped directly into a shaft of light coming through the window, the moonlight illuminating her body in its pale glow. She stopped there and simply let him look. She heard his sharp intake of breath, and knew he was doing just that. He had to be able to see her with crystal clarity.

He suddenly rolled back over, lunging to his feet on the other side of the bed. She saw that he wore only a pair of shorts, the garment hanging low on his waist, the fabric clinging to his thighs. When he came to his feet, he stood in profile for the slightest of moments, long enough for her to see the evidence of his arousal, hard and insistent, jutting before him. She almost smiled. This time there was no chance he could lie about it.

Then he turned back to the bed, facing her. He grabbed the sheet and whipped it off the mattress. Holding it open with both hands, he started toward her, arms extended, as though to cover her with it.

"You need to go back to bed."

"No, I don't. I need to be here."

He came within arm's length and tried to drape the sheet over her shoulders. She let her arms dangle at her sides, refusing to take the fabric or give it anything to catch on to. As soon as the cloth touched her shoulders, it immediately began to slip free, sliding downward.

With a frustrated groan, he moved closer, gripping the sheet tighter and holding it between them. She took a step of her own, closing the final distance. Her breasts brushed against his chest, the cloth between them so thin it might as well not have been there at all.

"Karina…" he began, his voice more thick with emotion than she'd ever heard.

"You want me here, too," she said.

Almost as soon as the words left her mouth, she reached up and grabbed the nearest end of the sheet. The motion was so sudden he didn't have time to tighten his hold on the fabric before she tore it out of his hands, letting it drift to the floor beside them.

And then there was nothing between them.

She waited for him to try to retreat, to take a step backward or to the side, prepared to follow, not about to let him try and escape.

He didn't move, his body completely frozen.

She tilted her head back, pushing up on her toes until their faces were mere inches apart, their mouths so very close to touching.

He started to shake his head weakly, never taking his eyes from hers. "We shouldn't—"

"Don't think about tomorrow. There is only tonight."

She didn't know if it was the words or her body pressed to his or just how close their mouths were. She didn't care. All that mattered was that an instant later he buried his mouth on hers.

The intensity of the kiss surprised her at first, just for a second. His lips moved against hers hard and fast and insistent, his tongue diving deep into her mouth. She quickly responded, hurrying to catch up, to take every taste and feel and sensation she could get.

Then his arms were around her, pulling her tight against his body. She sucked in a gasp, the sound swallowed by his mouth. Her breasts mashed, rubbed against the soft hair on his chest, the friction increasing the ache of her already-sensitive nipples. His arms were locked around her, firm and unyielding, and she basked in the feeling, the closeness and the urgency of his embrace.

She felt herself moving backward, her feet completely off the floor, then her back striking something solid. She distantly registered that they must have hit the wall. He tore his mouth away from hers to bury it against her neck. She raised her arms and slid her hands over his sides and the bottom of his back. He was so hard, so firm, his skin toned and tight and hot to the touch. He felt so good. What he was doing felt so good. But there was more. She instinctively knew that, the ache in her belly crying out for something else, something more.

Her hands dipped into the waistband of his shorts, dragging them lower, her fingers trailing along his buttocks. She knew the instant his erection was free, the thick fullness suddenly there against her body, pressing firmly, hardness against softness.

She barely had time to absorb the feel of him there. Almost immediately he slid his hands down her sides, grabbed her hips in both hands and thrust into her. There was no hesitation, no preparation, no warning. There was no need. Her body was already wet and ready and waiting for him. Even as he buried himself in her, she threw her head back, hitting it against the wall behind her as a low, breathy moan burst from her mouth. She hardly felt the impact, didn't even notice any pain. There was only him, inside her, around her.

For a moment after that initial thrust, he remained utterly still, sighing heavily, the sound nearly a moan like her own. She tightened her muscles around him, gripping him to her, drawing him in farther. He groaned against her neck, his breath hot against her skin, the sound shuddering through his body. She felt the vibration everywhere their bodies touched, all the way to her core.

Then he withdrew slightly and drove in again, deeper this time. Harder. Then again. She pushed her hips down to meet every thrust, wanting more. Their bodies moved in tandem, harder, faster with every stroke, gathering intensity by the moment. She felt the tension building, beneath her skin, deep in her belly, pushing higher and higher every time he drove into her, every time she drew him into her. She tried to hold back the inevitable release, tried to hold on to the feelings building inside her, better and fiercer and more wonderful than anything she'd ever experienced before. She wanted it to last as long as it could, even as it became harder to hold on, even as the promise of that sweet release became impossible to resist.

She felt him let go just as she did, his body tensing even further, one last time, at that final moment. They erupted together in a great liquid rush. As though from a great distance, she heard a cry of release burst from his mouth. It was drowned out by the sound of her own, the scream torn from her throat. Together they rode wave after wave, as he emptied himself inside her, as she erupted around him, again and again and again.

Finally, both an eternity later yet far too soon, she felt herself coming out of that delicious haze. Other sensations sank in. The wall behind her back. The sweat drenching her skin, and his. Luke, still buried inside her, his body still hard and tense, his arms locked around her.

She wrapped her arms around him and held on tightly, clinging to the feelings as long as she could. The feeling of this moment, of being here with him. The feeling of the blood rushing through her body, her heart pounding in her chest. The feeling of his racing just as fast, moving in sync with hers.

The feeling of living.

Of being alive.

Chapter Thirteen

Karina woke slowly, drifting up from the warm cocoon she found herself in. Her entire body felt at peace, satisfied and deeply content in a way she hadn't felt in a long time, if ever.

She tried to linger there as long as possible, until she could no longer deny that she was awake, even if her eyes remained closed. Gradually, she let her lids slide open.

And found herself looking straight into Luke's face.

Her heart immediately began to beat faster, adrenaline surging through her system as a flood of memories came over her. They lay side by side, facing each other. His arm was slung loosely over her hip, the only place where they were touching. There was something possessive about the gesture, as though he was holding her to him.

She peered up into his face, unguarded in sleep. A curious warmth she had no business feeling bloomed in her chest. She now knew more than ever how wrong she'd been when she first met him. This wasn't a man who felt nothing. If anything, he felt too much. That was why he tried to feel nothing. If he let himself love, it would be strong and fierce and unyielding.

But he would not let himself, she thought with a pang of sadness. Last night had not changed that. And even if he did, there was no reason to believe it would have anything to do with her.

He slowly exhaled, the sound indicating he was on the verge of waking. Nervousness fluttered in her belly, and she wondered if she should glance away or close her eyes so he wouldn't know she'd been watching him.

Before she could decide, his eyes slowly blinked open.

For a long moment, he simply looked at her, his gaze cloudy with sleep, his expression unguarded. She was almost able to pretend that his was the gaze of a man in love, staring deeply, endlessly, into the eyes of a woman he loved.

And then she saw the exact moment when he remembered. Who she was. What had happened. His brow furrowed slightly, his face hardened. His eyes drifted shut again, and it almost seemed as though he'd cringed.

"Morning," he said. His voice was rough with sleep, but not so much that she missed the uneasy note in it. He began to turn away from her, flopping over onto his back on the mattress.

"Good morning." She quickly rolled away from him, too, pushing herself up with one arm and swinging her legs over the side of the bed.

She reached for the sheet crumpled on the floor and wrapped it around herself, tucking the end in above her breasts to hold it in place. It seemed strange to feel so modest after her actions last night, but these were far different circumstances, and she felt the need for every protective covering she could find. Moving around the end of the bed, she headed for the door.

She'd almost made it when he stopped her.

"Karina."

She was almost tempted to keep walking, not wanting to hear what he had to say, not wanting him to ruin what had happened between them, what she would like to keep as a nice memory.

But he would know why she had ignored him, and it would only make things that much more uncomfortable, killing the memory as effectively as anything he could say.

She glanced back over her shoulder.

And immediately wished she hadn't.

He had sat up on the mattress, the blanket draped over his waist. She wasn't alone in her modesty. His expression was once again fixed in that cool, emotionless mask. She read the emotion in the slump of his shoulders just the same.

Regret.

His words confirmed it. "I'm sorry."

"Why?"

"I shouldn't have…"

"You didn't do anything I didn't want."

"Perhaps," he said with clear reluctance. "But one of us should have remembered the reality of our situation. It will make it more difficult to terminate the marriage now that it's been consummated. We may not be able to get an annulment."

"No one has to know. Or we can divorce."

"And you'd be okay with that?"

No, her mind rebelled. She was not okay with any of this. "That was the agreement. We will terminate the marriage. We did not say how."

"And that won't be a problem for you after last night?" he pressed.

She forced a smile. "It was one night. Nothing more."

She started to turn away again.

"We didn't use anything."

It took her a moment to understand what he was referring to, then she realized he was right. They hadn't used any kind of protection. It had seemed unimportant in the heat of the moment. Thinking of it would have meant thinking about the implications, what might happen, the future. And that was not what last night had been about.

She felt a strange hope pierce her heart. For just a moment, she let herself forget the reality of their situation, as he had put it, what it would mean to bring a child into this, to place an innocent life in danger. She thought only of the child. The baby she'd always wanted but long ago accepted she would never have. The baby she might be having now.

Except she knew her body, and she knew how unlikely that would be. The timing was not right.

She ruthlessly pushed back that feeling of anticipation, swallowing the ridiculous disappointment. It was better this way, of course. For all of them.

"Don't worry," she said. "It doesn't matter. The time is not right."

He exhaled slowly and nodded. She couldn't tell whether he was relieved or something else. She supposed it didn't matter.

She turned back toward the door. This time he didn't stop her.

She felt his eyes on her with every step. She held her head high and kept her shoulders relaxed, not about to give him reason to believe she felt anything different from what she'd told him. He wasn't the only one who could hide what he was feeling, she thought, even as another stab of longing she couldn't quite deny, for what had happened between them, for the closeness they'd shared, struck home.

It was one night, she reminded herself as firmly as she had him. Nothing more. There was no reason to dream of a future when she didn't know if she had one.

And no matter what else happened, she knew there was no future to be had with him.

LUKE STOPPED OUTSIDE the kitchen and tried to brace himself. He could hear Karina moving around inside, the soft scrape of her feet on the linoleum, the clink of glasses or dishware bumping against something solid. He could picture her in there, and the thought alone was enough to reignite the feelings he'd been trying to tamp down from the moment he'd woken that morning and found himself looking into her eyes.

He'd showered for a good half hour. She must have used up all the hot water, because it had already been lukewarm when he'd stepped beneath the spray. He hadn't cared, remaining in there long after it had turned outright cold. It hadn't helped, no matter how long he'd waited, no matter how hard he'd tried not to forget.

He could still hear the sound of her moaning his name in the back of his mind.

Luka, she'd groaned, her accent thick in those heated moments.

His eyes sank shut at the memory, at the images that accompanied it, the sensations that burned along his nerve endings as though he were living it again.

Damn. He shook his head in a failed attempt to clear it. He'd known he'd dug a hole for himself where this woman was concerned. But last night he'd allowed things to go much further than he ever should have. Now there was no escaping that.

Some part of him couldn't regret it no matter how much he wanted to.

Not that he could let her know that.

He took a long, deep breath, then stepped into the room.

Karina stood at the counter, sipping from a coffee mug. She was wearing a pullover on top of a T-shirt, the clothes baggy enough that they should have hidden her curves. It didn't matter. He remembered each one, remembered every line and swell of her body as clearly as if she was standing before him bare.

The corner of his mouth twitched at the thought, the only part of him that betrayed his emotions.

He had it back under control by the time she looked up to meet his eyes.

"I made coffee," she said unnecessarily, the aroma of it having already reached his nose.

"Thank you."

She automatically moved away from the counter and toward the table, giving him a wide berth. For his benefit or her own?

He looked away, registering that she must be taking a seat at the sound of the chair being pulled away from the table. Reaching for the pot, he poured himself a cup, then leaned back against the counter and took a long swallow. The coffee was hot, burning as it went down. He didn't care.

"What do we do now?" she asked.

He managed to keep from swallowing hard or reacting at all to the question. Damn. He should have known she wouldn't be able to let what had happened last night go without comment.

He turned and looked at her. "What do you mean?" he asked calmly.

"Should we go somewhere else or do you want to stay here longer?"

Of course. She'd made it clear last night had meant nothing to her, no matter how hard he found that to believe. Whether she believed it or insisted on pretending, there was no reason she would bring it up.

"We should be safe here for a little while longer, at least until tomorrow." No matter how much he longed to leave the place and the memories it now contained. "I'll think of somewhere we can head tomorrow."

"And then what? Another place after that? And another after that?"

No, of course not, he realized. They couldn't simply run indefinitely. Eventually he'd have to go back to work. He had a job, a life. One he needed to return to, he thought with a certain amount of relief. They'd been fortunate enough to have all of this happen at a time when he'd been able to clear his calendar, but that was very much a temporary situation. As he'd told her, his career typically occupied most of his time. He had to remain married to her, but that didn't mean they had to be together around the clock. He'd been wrong to think he had to personally keep her safe. He could hire security guards to watch over her. He could go back to his life and their marriage could go back to being in name only, the way it was originally intended to be.

"No, we'll have to go back to Baltimore eventually. I'll beef up the security at the house, and if it can't be made safe enough, I'll either hire security guards or I can find a new place. Maybe an apartment in a building with restricted access where they won't be able to get to you." Even though he'd lived in his house for years, the idea hardly bothered him. It had never been more than a place to sleep and occasionally eat, purchased as an investment more than anything else.

"And I will hide forever."

The bleakness in the statement brought an end to his growing excitement over the plans he'd been forming. She looked at him, a sad smile on her face. "It is what I expected."

"Not forever," he insisted. "Until we figure out a way to end this."

"There is only one way this can end."

"That's right."

The words were blunt, harsh. But what was most disturbing was that neither he nor Karina had said them.

And Luke knew who had, recognizing the voice immediately, even as shock and disbelief warred inside him, saying it wasn't even remotely possible.

But when he turned to the doorway, he saw it wasn't only possible, it was actually happening.

Anton Solokov stood in the entryway. Three men with guns aimed directly at Luke and Karina shuffled into position behind him. Solokov didn't have a weapon, but it didn't matter. One look in his eyes and it was clear he was the most dangerous of them all.

"You will give me back what is mine, Karina Andreevna," he said, the barely contained rage in his tone sending a jolt through Luke.

"And then we will end this once and for all."

Chapter Fourteen

It was her worst nightmare come to life.

Solokov. Here.

And there was nowhere to run.

And like many nightmares, it made no sense. That feeling that everything was unreal came over her again. How could he be there? How had he found them?

Karina stared at the man, unable to move, unable to do anything. She'd met him before, only once in passing. Dmitri had introduced them. The encounter hadn't lasted long enough to provide a firm impression, but she remembered that even then something about him had made her uneasy.

It was nothing compared to the terror that ripped along her nerve endings now, holding her frozen.

She somehow managed to speak. "How did you find us?"

He raised a brow. "How could we not? Your directions were quite accurate. You simply did not expect us to get here so soon, before you could lay your trap, did you?"

The words made no sense. She shook her head in confusion. "What are you talking about? What directions?"

A trace of impatience flashed across his genial expression. "Come now. There is no more reason to play games. We all know the truth here." His eyes widened slightly. "Or do we? Could it be he really doesn't know the truth about you?"

"What truth?" Luke demanded.

Solokov barked out a laugh, the sound scraping at her nerves. "You really are just a pawn. She called me three days ago and informed me she would sell me the numbers for the offshore accounts where Dmitri put the money he stole from me. She said too many people had been hurt, said she had all the account numbers. She just didn't know how to touch them herself without drawing attention to herself, so they did her no good. She offered to sell them to me for plain cash."

She could only shake her head in disbelief. "That is not true. I did not call you."

His mouth twisted with annoyance. "I told you to stop playing games. Now everyone here really does know the truth."

She glanced at Luke, unsure of what she would see. Would he believe the man's lies?

His face had hardened, revealing nothing as usual. "When exactly did you receive this call?" he asked.

"Three days ago. Just after your wedding."

"And after your men shot Viktor Yevchenko."

"She may have mentioned something about an unfortunate incident, about not wanting anyone else to be hurt." His tone and his smirk said the idea amused him.

"Karina was with me the entire time."

"Are you so certain of that? She was never out of your sight? Never stepped into the bathroom where you couldn't see or hear what she was doing?"

"I would have noticed if she'd taken the phone with her and she didn't have a cell phone at the time."

"That you know of," Solokov said. "I suspect there are still many things you do not know about this woman."

"If you thought she wanted to make a deal, why did you still have your men break into my house?"

"A regrettable mistake. I was unable to reach them in time and they acted on their own." He shot an indulgent glance at Karina. "I thought you might change your mind then, but you did not."

"I never called you," Karina repeated.

"Who else would contact me with such an offer? Who else would tell me where you were?"

It was a good question. She couldn't imagine who would do such a thing, or why. She didn't even know how anyone could know where they were. She only knew that it had not been her who summoned this man.

"Why didn't this person offer to e-mail the information and have you wire the money somewhere?" Luke asked.

"Because she knew I was not going to risk losing more of my money without assurance that she would give me the information. The exchange had to be conducted in person."

"Whose idea was it to meet in person, yours or the other person?"

"It was hers. She refused to give the information to anyone but me."

"And this person told you to come here?" Luke asked.

"Yes, this afternoon."

"And you came even though you thought it might be a trap?"

"That is why we came early. A wise decision, it would seem. We searched the entire farm. You did not have time to get your people into place. I am certain if we had come at the requested time there would have been many people here."

"I promise you Karina did not call you," Luke said, his voice ringing with conviction. "Now I don't know who it was, but if I were you, I would seriously be wondering why that person was so desperate to meet you in person and direct you here."

For just a moment Solokov's brow furrowed, as he seemed to consider Luke's words. Then he shook his head. "You are an attorney, are you not? I can see you are good one. But you are wasting your time. Do not try to distract me. It will do you no good."

He turned to Karina. "Now, you promised to return my money to me. Of course I promised to pay you for the information, but arrangements can be negotiated. Instead I am going to kill you. But it can be fast or it can be slow and painful, depending on how difficult you want to be. The choice is yours. You only need to give me what I want."

"I don't have what you want."

"Difficult, then. That is your choice." With a contemptuous sneer, he turned slowly and surveyed the room. "This space is too small. We need more room for this. Take her to the barn."

The man standing behind Luke nudged him with his weapon. "What about him? Do you want me to kill him?" The excitement in his voice left little doubt what he hoped the answer would be.

No. The horrified scream rose in her throat, but the terror that gripped her was so fierce that her muscles wouldn't release the sound. She couldn't even turn her head. She could only glance at Luke, her eyes going wide.

He remained as emotionless as ever, despite the man or his words or the gun poised to kill. Not a muscle moved on his face. He stared steadily at Solokov, a hint of defiance in the way he simply looked at the man, as though he didn't care what his judgment was.

Karina jerked her gaze back to Solokov. He hadn't answered. He was looking at her, his eyes now narrowed slightly. Something in them sent a fresh unease crawling up her spine.

"No," he said, finally giving voice to the word still shrieking through her mind. "Bring him. He may be useful."

To threaten her with, she realized warily. He'd seen how much the idea of something happening to Luke had terrified her. She'd made the mistake of letting this man know what she felt for Luke, and he knew he could use it against her. That was the reason for the reprieve, however temporary.

Because he thought he could do far worse than killing him.

Because of her.

All the scenarios she'd contemplated the past two months of what they might do to her once they caught her came rushing to the surface. Except now they weren't being done to her. They were being done to Luke.

Almost as though he'd read her mind, Solokov reached over into a block of knives on the counter and pulled one out, its blade gleaming in the morning sunlight. He held it up, seeming to test the feel of it in his hand, and smiled.

"Yes," he said, almost to himself. "He may be very useful."

THEY WERE LED TO THE BARN at the same time, one of Solokov's men behind each of them, Solokov and the remaining man tailing behind. Karina kept her eyes on Luke's back, knowing the man behind him must have his gun pressed to Luke's spine, as the man behind her did to her.

When they entered the barn, she began to move to where Luke's captor had led him. The man behind her pushed his gun deeper into her back, nudging her in the other direction. "Over there."

She had no choice but to do as he ordered. She didn't think he would shoot her, not even a nonlethal shot, not yet. But any of them could shoot Luke to force her to cooperate. It was exactly as Solokov had intended.

No, she thought with a shudder, remembering the knife. He intended far more than that.

Solokov finally stepped into the barn, his eyes immediately going to a few old wooden chairs stacked up in the corner. "Bring two chairs," he instructed the man beside him.

The man quickly complied. He brought them to where Solokov stood. Solokov jerked his head toward the opening behind them. "Keep watch outside. Make sure no one else comes."

The man obeyed with a sharp nod, disappearing into the bright morning sunlight.

Picking up one of the chairs, Solokov carried it several yards from the other, situating it so that the two chairs were facing one another. After glancing between them a few times, he appeared satisfied with their location. He looked at Karina and gestured to the chair beside him with the knife. "Sit."

Karina had no time to hesitate or choose whether to obey. The man behind her drove his gun into her back, forcing her forward. She stumbled to the chair and dropped into the seat.

Solokov had already moved away from it, heading back to the other chair. He must have given Luke's captor a silent order, because the man's hand was on Luke's shoulder, forcing him into the seat. Luke's posture was straight and clearly unwilling as he fell into it.

Their eyes met. He had to know what they intended

to do to him as well as she did. There was no sign of it on his face, of course. He nodded subtly to her, a small sign of encouragement, but otherwise didn't react.

For the first time, she envied his coolness. She wished she too could bury her feelings so effectively, swallow her fear about what was happening and what might happen still. Instead it seemed to fill every cell in her body, causing her heart to pound hard against her chest, her throat to close up.

Luke's captor had moved a few feet away. Solokov had taken his place beside Luke, the knife still gripped tightly in his right hand. He dropped his left on Luke's shoulder. Luke didn't blink, didn't flinch, didn't give any indication he'd noticed.

"Now, Karina Andreevna, I have come all this way. You will tell me where my money is."

Despite the way he'd chosen to address her, he otherwise spoke in English. Because he wanted to be sure Luke understood every word? Was he so determined to play out this sick game, to convince Luke she had betrayed him? But to what purpose? Was he simply that twisted?

She met his eyes directly, hoping against hope he could see the truth in them. "Please. I truly do not know anything about the money."

His jaw tensing, he stepped slightly forward. "It is time to stop lying. For every lie you continue to tell, your husband will be punished. The choice is yours."

She'd known this was what he intended, why he'd let Luke live, why he'd brought them both to the barn. Still, hearing him say it sent fresh terror ripping through her. Her gaze flicked to Luke. He gave no sign he was at all affected by Solokov's words.

Karina refocused on Solokov. "I swear to you I don't know."

She didn't even finish the sentence. With no warning he raised the knife and plunged it into Luke's thigh.

She couldn't even gasp. The shock, the horror, of it was too severe. Her mouth fell open, gaping silently as she stared at the blade half-buried in Luke's leg, Solokov's hand wrapped around the handle so tightly his knuckles were white.

A low cry of pain burst from Luke's mouth. Almost immediately, he clamped his lips shut, and she could see the words working against them.

Solokov pulled out the knife, the metal making a sickening sound as it was withdrawn from Luke's flesh. His face clenched in pain, Luke slowly moved his hand to the fresh wound and pressed down on it. She watched him gradually regain his control, tears filling her eyes. The effort played across his face, but eventually, his expression smoothed. He looked straight ahead, not meeting her eyes.

The gleam of metal drew her eye to the knife Solokov still held, the blade now dripping blood. She raised her gaze to find him watching her, his brow arched.

"You are wasting my time," he said, his tone carrying an edge as sharp as the knife in his hand. "Where is my money?"

She froze, not wanting to answer, not knowing what

else she could do. She knew only one answer to give, but to do so would only cause Luke to be hurt further. She tried to think of a lie, something to at least delay what might happen. Her mind refused to cooperate, her thoughts damnably slow.

"Tell me," Solokov said.

She felt the tears spill over, pouring down her cheeks. She made no move to wipe them away, her body frozen in terror. There wasn't the slightest indication on his face that he was impacted by them in the least. His expression remained cold and unrelenting.

She sensed his impatience building like a gathering storm. She had to swallow several times to force out the words. "I don't know," she said, little more than a barely audible whisper.

Even as she said them, she braced herself for what might happen next, fully anticipating something as shocking in its suddenness as his last action.

Solokov didn't move at all. He simply stared at her, his eyes narrowing to thin slits. He said nothing. After a while, that became even more terrifying than anything he could have done, the uncertainty making the wait ever more unbearable.

Finally, he turned. Her pulse jumped as he began to walk around Luke.

"It appears I was wrong about what this man means to you. Perhaps I had no reason to keep him alive or bring him out here at all. If you do not care about what happens to him, then he is of no use to me."

He stopped directly behind Luke and turned to face

her. In the next instant, he grabbed a fistful of hair from the top of Luke's head and placed the still-bloody blade to Luke's throat.

Her heart stopped. She felt it. One second it pulsed, the next it did not. Everything seemed to freeze with it. The horrible scene before her. The two men locked in the hideous pose. She could not even blink.

Then Solokov began speaking again. Her heart jumped back into action, faster this time, creeping higher in her throat with every panicked throb.

"One last time," Solokov said. "Tell me where my money is."

Once again she froze. Her mouth fell open on its own, working silently, forming words she was unable to utter. She wanted to scream, to beg, to cry, but was too terrified to do any of them, too afraid to risk saying, doing the wrong thing.

She knew only one answer to give. And she knew it was the wrong one.

She looked at Luke, staring resolutely ahead, only the vein throbbing furiously at his neck, directly above the knife, betraying what he was feeling. She wished she could apologize for involving him in this. She wished she could say how sorry she was for what was about to happen.

She wished she could say how much he had come to mean to her, in spite of everything, in such a short amount of time.

Her attention locked on Luke's face, she almost missed the sudden jerk of the knife against his throat.

Her gaze dropped, her mouth falling open entirely in

a silent scream. She watched for the gush of blood, for Luke's life to come pouring out of him.

Then she realized the blade hadn't pierced the skin. Solokov's hand had simply spasmed.

No, Solokov had spasmed, she thought in disbelief, as the man suddenly began to fall over, the movement almost seeming to happen in slow motion.

Moments later, Solokov fell to the ground, the knife clattering to the floor beside him. He didn't move again.

Then similar sounds, like the one of Solokov hitting the ground that she'd barely begun to process, reached her ears. The flash of motion out of the corner of her eye drew her attention just behind Luke, where one of Solokov's men had stood. He, too, was facedown on the ground. She jerked her head behind her, suddenly realizing she no longer felt the hovering presence of the man who'd been there. He, too, was on the ground, his eyes open and staring blindly at the roof. And she knew he was dead.

Once again, everything seemed unreal. *Dead,* she thought numbly. Solokov was dead. His men were dead. How—

The soft crunch of footsteps on the packed dirt floor made her look back toward the open barn doors.

Viktor stepped out of the bright sunlight into the interior of the barn. The gun he still braced in both hands answered exactly what had just happened.

"Viktor," she sighed with relief, with gratitude.

Brow furrowed, Luke started to rise from his chair, then stopped, glancing down to where his hand was still pressed to his thigh.

At the sight, Karina rose on unsteady legs, automatically pulling off her shirt, leaving on the T-shirt underneath. "Luke," she said, still breathless. She moved toward him, quickly tying the shirt tightly around his wound to stop the bleeding.

When she was done, she looked up to meet his eyes. His brow was dotted with sweat, no doubt from the pain of his injury and strain of keeping his emotions in check the past several minutes. Now a hint of emotion, something she couldn't quite read, glowed in his eyes. She could only stare back, overcome with relief that they were both here, both alive.

After a moment, Luke rose all the way and turned to face Viktor. "The man outside?"

"Dead, too."

"How did you find us?"

"There are tracking chips embedded in each of your wedding rings."

Luke frowned. "Why?"

"So I'd know where you were." Viktor jerked a shoulder at Solokov. "Because of this."

The answer didn't seem to satisfy Luke. If anything his frown deepened. She couldn't imagine why. She had too much happiness, too much relief, emotions she'd never thought she would feel again, surging through her body. She was nearly giddy from it.

Then it hit her. Yes, if Solokov was dead, then it truly was over. All of it. Her excitement began to waver, uncertainty rushing in to take its place.

Luke turned and looked at her.

And for just a moment, she thought she saw his face begin to soften, his mouth easing, as though he was about to smile.

Then something struck her, hard and unrelenting, in her belly. The impact rocked her body, knocked the breath from her lungs. The shock of it gripped her from head to toe.

Then there was pain, sharp and agonizing, in her abdomen. She pressed a hand to her side, her fingers instantly coming into contact with wetness. Dazed, puzzled, she lifted her hand to find it covered in redness.

Blood, she thought distantly. *I am bleeding.*

Still not understanding, she raised her head, forcing her eyes to focus on the man in front of her.

Viktor, standing there, his gun still aimed.

At her.

Viktor had shot her.

It didn't make sense. He stared at her without emotion, the same look she'd seen on Luke's face so many times.

Luke.

She instinctively began to glance back at him. Her gaze was already swimming before it reached him, her legs suddenly feeling boneless. She blinked to try to regain her vision, attempted to clear a mind that suddenly seemed to have gone foggy.

It was too late.

The last thing she saw was the barn's rafters high above her before they, too, faded into blackness.

Chapter Fifteen

Luke didn't understand at first what had just happened. One moment Karina was standing there, smiling at him. Then her eyes went wide, her mouth falling slightly open. He followed her gaze as she lowered it to her hand, the palm now drenched in blood. Blood from the wound at her side.

And the silenced gunshot he'd heard moments earlier, the sound more faint than silent, finally registered in his mind.

Just before Karina's eyes rolled back in her head and she collapsed to the ground.

A surge of pain, so raw and agonizing it nearly drove him to his knees, ripped through him. He couldn't even force out her name through a throat frozen in horror. She lay there, still and unmoving. The wound on her lower abdomen slowly grew, the stain of blood spreading.

He started to lean forward, his body primed to lurch toward her on legs gone wooden. At the last second, some instinctive part of him recognized what was happening and took over. He whipped his head toward Viktor.

Viktor who still had his gun raised, now aimed at Luke.

Viktor who stared back, an expression strangely like triumph glowing feverishly in his eyes.

Even as Luke watched uncomprehendingly, the other man's mouth began to curve upward in a smile.

It didn't make any sense. After everything he'd done to save Karina, after all the concern he'd exhibited—

The words came out on their own, hoarse with confusion and disbelief. "What the hell are you doing?"

"Avenging my father."

"You did that already. Solokov is dead."

"And now so is the person who got my father killed."

It felt like his brain was incapable of forming a single coherent thought. "But you said you wanted to save her. You went to the trouble of convincing me to marry her to protect her."

"Because I needed her here, as bait to lure Solokov. There was no way I could get close enough to him in Russia to punish him for having my father killed. I needed to bring him here, where I could control the situation. And for that, I needed her."

Realization dawned. "You told him where to find us. You led him here to trap him."

"With the assistance of a female friend who has no trouble slipping back into her native Russian accent and who also has cause to hate Solokov. Tending to bullet wounds isn't her only talent. He found her quite convincing." He gestured around the barn with his free hand. "You really did choose the perfect location. For that, I thank you."

It was all Luke could do not to launch himself at the man to knock the damned smirk off his face. His anger seemed to have jolted his brain back into awareness. He finally understood the feeling he'd had that something didn't make sense. On the phone Viktor had said he didn't want to know where they were. But why say that if he had the capability to know where they were the whole time thanks to the rings he himself had provided? The only possible reason was that he didn't want them to know, wanted them completely unaware.

As it appeared they had been. About so many things.

His eyes returned to Karina. She appeared to still be breathing, her chest rising and falling the slightest bit. The motion was so subtle he almost wondered if his mind was playing tricks on him, providing him with what he desperately wanted to see.

He turned his full attention to Viktor, damn well ready to beg if necessary. "Please, Viktor. You don't want to do this. You're not a killer."

The smirk only deepened. "I think Solokov and his men would disagree with you on that."

"They were killers. Karina is innocent. She didn't do anything wrong."

"She brought danger to my father's doorstep," he spat. "She knew exactly who was after her, what they would do to get to her, and she did it anyway."

"And all that business about protecting her? You had me really believing you wanted me to."

"Oh, I really did. I needed her safe and out of Solokov's hands until the situation was arranged to my advantage. Not to mention I didn't know if there might be any other interested parties who would come after her in hopes of learning what she knew about the money. It wouldn't have done me any good if you'd let him or anyone else get to her before I could have him where I wanted him. Until they both could pay."

"Revenge won't bring back your father."

"No, but it feels very good." He smiled. "I learned that long ago."

Something in the way Viktor smiled at him, something in the unsettling glow in his eyes, sent a warning through Luke's system. "What do you mean by that?"

"I mean you, of course." The smile twisted, the nastiness underlying it rising to the surface. "And Melanie."

Everything inside Luke went very still. "What about Melanie?"

"I loved her, did you know that? I loved her from the first moment I saw her. And then I made the mistake of introducing her to you. After that, all she saw was you. You stole her from me." He shook his head. "I hated you both so much. Her for acting like I'd never existed to her, you for taking her away. But never more than that night at the party. The two of you were sickening. Staring at each other. Falling all over each other. I wanted you to hurt as much as I did."

"You're the one who hit us that night," he said numbly.

"You were both supposed to die, not just her. But you

didn't. You lived. And I realized it was much more satisfying to watch you suffer than to have you die."

"You got off on watching me mourn Melanie, you sick bastard?"

"Oh, not just Melanie. That wasn't nearly enough. After all, I lost her, too. You needed to lose more. And so you did."

Horror washed over him, the idea so terrible his mind tried to reject it even as he knew it had to be true. "You killed my parents."

"And then you finally suffered the way you deserved." Viktor shook his head slowly with faux sympathy. "Poor Luke, all alone. Which worked out perfectly when this situation arose and I needed someone to marry Karina. I thought it would be enough to force you to lose another wife, since she was always going to die. I just never realized you were going to fall in love with her."

Luke started. "I don't know what you're talking about."

"Come now. It was written all over your face. The way you looked at her just before I shot her. I remember that look. Never thought I'd see it again. Never thought I wanted to see it again. Until I did. You love her."

Luke wanted to deny it. He should deny it, for both their sakes. He opened his mouth to do just that.

The words failed to come. Instead, he could only stand there, mouth open, barely seeing the man before him, as the realization struck him hard enough that he almost rocked back on his heels.

He did feel…something for this woman. She'd made it happen, made him feel things he didn't want to. She'd challenged him, broken down every last defense. She'd crawled beneath his skin and worked her way into his—

Not heart. He couldn't bring himself to even think that. Whatever he felt for her, it was different from what he'd felt for Melanie, what he'd believed to be love. That had been amazing, but simple and sweet. What he felt for Karina was complicated and intense.

But no less amazing.

He didn't know if it was love. He damn well didn't want it to be. But he did know he cared about this woman, on a level that went far beyond simple concern for the life of another human being. She meant something to him.

She meant a hell of a lot to him.

Viktor smiled.

"And now you're going to stand here and watch her die."

Luke stared at the man before him, unable to believe he'd been so blind. That thought he'd had when Viktor had first brought Karina to him, that this man was not his friend, came roaring back. Had he somehow known the truth, on a deeper level than he'd realized at that moment? Maybe he had. Just as he knew something now.

"No."

Viktor's anger momentarily gave way to confusion. "No?"

"No," Luke said more firmly, practically a snarl. "I'm not going to play your sick game. You don't have any leverage."

"I'll shoot you."

"But if you kill me, that'll end the game, won't it?"

Viktor lowered his weapon to Luke's midsection. The same area where he'd shot Karina, Luke realized, anger and tension warring within him. "Not if I choose my shot well. You can live long enough to watch her die first."

"Unless I pass out from the pain. The way she has," he tossed out. He had no idea if it was true. He couldn't risk taking his eyes off Viktor, couldn't give the bastard the satisfaction of knowing he cared deeply enough to check on her status for a single instant no matter how badly every instinct screamed to know how she was. He could only hope the comment caused Viktor to lose focus for just a second, draw his attention to Karina so Luke could make a move.

But Viktor's steady gaze never wavered. As he'd said, this wasn't really about her. It was about Luke.

"She's a woman," Viktor spat. "Weak. Of course she would pass out sooner. You won't be so lucky."

Damn it. This was taking too long.

Luke extended his arms, making himself an open target.

"Then do it. Shoot me."

He braced himself. Waiting for it. Needing something to happen.

Viktor didn't take the shot. Indecision flickered across his face.

Luke knew exactly what he was thinking. The bastard wanted this too badly. Had wanted it for years. He was too afraid of making the wrong choice, doing something to jeopardize the vengeance he'd sought for years.

The moment of indecision cost him.

Luke had no such trouble taking action. He dropped to the ground, simultaneously rolling and sending his legs flying out toward Viktor. The bastard's legs were knocked right out from under him.

And then Luke was on top of him, his hand already closed in a fist before he even drew back his arm.

Viktor had barely begun to shift his head toward Luke when the first blow landed. It was quickly followed by another, then another. Luke didn't feel any of them. He only noticed the blood that came flying from Viktor's mouth and nose. He only saw the pain that crumpled the bastard's face, the way his eyes soon cringed, then closed completely, then didn't open again. He only knew the rage and fury and pure agony exploding in his mind and body and soul, feelings more raw and real than anything he'd allowed himself to feel in years and didn't have any hope of burying. He could only keep striking this sick bastard who'd stolen so much from him.

He thought of Melanie.

He thought of his parents.

He thought of Karina.

Karina.

The realization came slowly, the knowledge that Viktor was unconscious and likely had been a half-dozen blows earlier. Blood dripped from his nose and mouth. His eyes were closed, his lips gaping.

Luke had to force himself to stop, fighting every impulse that wanted him to keep on hitting Viktor until there was nothing left to hit. He made himself focus on the reason for what he was doing.

Karina.

Gradually, with painstaking effort, his arm responded, the blows coming slower, with less force behind them. Until he was able to stop completely.

As soon as he did, he pushed off from Viktor, gazing around wildly for Karina. Spotting her, he staggered toward her prone form. He gave a brief thought to getting Viktor's gun so the man wouldn't have it when he regained consciousness. Part of him acknowledged that wasn't going to happen for a long time.

And then he was at her side, his eyes pouring over her, Viktor forgotten. He felt a small twinge of relief that he hadn't been imagining things earlier. She was still breathing. But her breathing was shallow and uneven. And she was bleeding. God, there was so much blood.

He quickly lifted her in his arms, wincing at the pain in his injured leg as he rose to his feet. He swallowed it back and moved forward, stumbling at first, then gaining momentum and strength with every step. There was no time to wait for an ambulance. He knew where the closest hospital was, had passed by it on his way through the nearest town.

"You're going to be okay," he murmured, even though he knew there was little chance she could consciously hear the words. But maybe some part of her deep inside would know, would feel his presence and be comforted by it.

But mostly the words were for him. Because he

needed to hear them, needed to believe them. Needed to know he wasn't going to lose her.

She was going to be okay.

She had to be.

Chapter Sixteen

Seven days in the hospital should have left Karina more than ready to leave. She didn't like the place. It was stark and sterile and cold. She didn't like being surrounded by strangers, didn't like how the place felt in the dark of the night when it was so quiet and still, with only the beep of the machines and faint whispers to fill the silence.

But on the eighth day, the day she was to leave, she felt only dread and sadness as she watched the gaping doorway, waiting for Luke to arrive.

The day was finally here. Time to go.

If only she knew where she was going, or what she would do now.

Luke had been there every day, but had not said a word about the future. Neither had she. Now that she had a future, she was still too afraid to think about it, though for different reasons than before.

Luke. She closed her eyes at the stab of pain the mere thought of him inspired.

The first time she'd woken in the hospital, she'd

seen him asleep in the chair by her bed. He'd looked terrible, still dressed in the shirt he'd been wearing that awful day on the farm, though someone must have provided him with a new pair of pants. The ones he was wearing didn't have any blood on them, and one leg bulged from what must have been the bandage on his wound beneath it. His hair was unkempt, his face unshaven, his expression rough and haggard. There'd been dark circles beneath his eyes. He'd looked like a man who hadn't slept in days and had finally collapsed from exhaustion, even though she'd later learned it had been only one day since everything that happened with Viktor and Solokov.

The fact that he'd been there, cared enough to remain by her bedside, had filled her with such a sense of lightness and hope that she'd been smiling when she closed her eyes again.

The next time she'd seen him, he'd been more the man she knew. He'd cleaned up, his demeanor was polite and reserved, and he never acknowledged that he'd ever been by her bedside.

And she'd known nothing had changed.

So it was time to move on.

Solokov and his men were dead, and with them, anyone to care about the money. Wherever Dmitri had put it was where it would likely remain, most likely adding to the balance sheet of some lucky banker somewhere. Karina never wanted to think about it again.

Viktor was in jail, where Luke assured her he would remain for a very long time, if not forever. She was almost glad Sergei was no longer alive to learn the kind of man his son was. Whoever Viktor's female accomplice had been, she seemed to have disappeared without a trace, no doubt satisfied now that Solokov was dead.

All the threats to her were gone. She was free.

It was time to live her life.

A life without him.

As if summoned by her thoughts, Luke suddenly filled the doorway of the hospital room. For a moment, she almost thought she saw a hint of uncertainty flash across his face as he looked at her.

Then it was gone. His expression was as cool and remote as ever.

"Are you ready to go?" he asked.

She rose to her feet, finding the courage to ask the question she'd needed to but had been too afraid to. "Where are you taking me?"

"I wasn't sure if you'd be comfortable at my place, but I hired a cleaning service to take care of the mess. I also had the security upgraded, not that I expect any trouble in the foreseeable future. But if you don't want to stay there, we can check into a hotel."

She frowned at him. "Why would *we* go to a hotel?"

He matched her frown. "Where did you think I would take you?"

"The embassy to make arrangements to leave, or to an attorney to sign any papers if you do not have them with you." She had figured he'd waited to give her the papers until after she was out of the hospital, a kindness as she recovered from the shooting. There had seemed to be no other reason why he would wait. She had thought he would be eager to end everything.

"You want to leave," he said, almost sounding surprised.

"There is no reason to stay anymore. We agreed to end the marriage when there was no more danger. Now it is over."

"It might look suspicious if we ended the marriage so soon."

"If you need to, you can say I tricked you into the marriage so you don't get in trouble. They will deport me, but that is not a problem anymore."

He swallowed. "Why don't you stay?"

Something in his voice, even more than the question, sent a flicker of hope through her. "Why?"

He didn't answer immediately, lowering his head.

Once again she thought of the man she'd seen at her bedside, the one who'd cared enough to stay with her through the night. She peered at him, desperately seeking some trace of that man in the one who stood before her.

Instead, all she saw was what he wanted her to, the man who hid himself, what he was feeling, if he allowed himself to feel anything at all.

She'd been married to a man who'd kept parts of his life hidden from her, who hadn't loved her enough. The reasons didn't matter. It was still the same. She couldn't do it again, couldn't love someone who couldn't be completely honest with her, couldn't be with someone incapable of loving with his whole heart, couldn't feel her love fade into bitterness and then nothing at all. No matter how much some sad part of her wanted to take as much as he would give as though it were better than nothing at all.

She shook her head. "I'm sorry," she said, a tremor in her voice. "I can't."

Unable to look at him, she started for the doorway. She didn't know where she was going. He was there to take her out of here. She only knew she couldn't look at him anymore.

She was halfway there when he caught her, capturing her arm and drawing her to a halt. She let him turn her around but kept her head lowered, bracing herself against whatever he might say.

He said nothing for a long moment. Then—

"Please. I don't want you to go."

Something in his voice, an odd note she'd never heard before, forced her to raise her head.

What she saw made the breath catch in her throat.

Pain. Misery. Desperation. Longing. They were all there, fighting for prominence. There was no trace of the coolness she was accustomed to seeing on his face. There was simply raw emotion.

For her.

"I love you," he said. "I know I've given you no reason to believe that, and it's probably crazy given the amount of time we've known each other. God knows I've spent the last week trying to convince myself it isn't true, because the idea scares the hell out of me. But I've spent too many years being too damned afraid to feel anything, and I know what I feel now. I didn't want to know it, but I do. I love you. I'd give anything for a fresh start, and if you give me a chance, I'll spend as long as you're willing to give to show you and see if you could love me, too."

Karina stared up into his eyes, almost unable to believe what she was seeing. From the moment she'd met him, she'd longed to see such true feeling from him, but now that she did, the sight tore at her heart. She reached up and placed her hands on his cheeks, wishing she could wipe away the agony she saw with her fingertips, smooth the pained lines with her touch.

"You just did," she whispered. "And I already do."

For a moment, he simply stared at her, a combination of hope and disbelief and absolute relief flashing across his face. His shoulders sagged, and a long, deep breath shuddered unsteadily from his lungs.

Then he reached forward and pulled her into his arms. He held her tightly against his body, his embrace just as she'd known his love would be: strong and fierce and unyielding. She wrapped her arms around his neck as he buried his face in her throat, holding him just as tightly as he did her. Closing her eyes, she let the essence of him surround her. His scent. His touch. The unsteady beating of his heart in his chest, racing as fast as her own.

This was it, she thought. Her future. Here at last.

And it was with him, after all.

* * * * *

Don't miss Kerry Connor's next book,
STRANGER IN A SMALL TOWN, on sale in 2010
and only in Harlequin Intrigue®.

*Celebrate 60 years of pure reading pleasure
with Harlequin®!
Just in time for the holidays,
Silhouette Special Edition® is proud to present
New York Times bestselling author
Kathleen Eagle's
ONE COWBOY, ONE CHRISTMAS*

Rodeo rider Zach Beaudry was a travelin' man—
until he broke down in middle-of-nowhere South
Dakota during a deep freeze. That's when an angel
came to his rescue....

"Don't die on me. Come on, Zel. You know how much I love you, girl. You're all I've got. Don't do this to me here. Not *now*."

But Zelda had quit on him, and Zach Beaudry had no one to blame but himself. He'd taken his sweet time hitting the road, and then miscalculated a shortcut. For all he knew he was a hundred miles from gas. But even if they were sitting next to a pump, the ten dollars he had in his pocket wouldn't get him out of South Dakota, which was not where he wanted to be right now. Not even his beloved pickup truck, Zelda, could get him much of anywhere on fumes. He was sitting out in the cold in the middle of nowhere. And getting colder.

He shifted the pickup into Neutral and pulled hard on the steering wheel, using the downhill slope to get her off the blacktop and into the roadside grass, where she shuddered to a standstill. He stroked the padded dash. "You'll be safe here."

But Zach would not. It was getting dark, and it was

already too damn cold for his cowboy ass. Zach's battered body was a barometer, and he was feeling South Dakota, big-time. He'd have given his right arm to be climbing into a hotel hot tub instead of a brutal blast of north wind. The right was his free arm anyway. Damn thing had lost altitude, touched some part of the bull and caused him a scoreless ride last time out.

It wasn't scoring him a ride this night, either. A carload of teenagers whizzed by, topping off the insult by laying on the horn as they passed him. It was at least twenty minutes before another vehicle came along. He stepped out and waved both arms this time, damn near getting himself killed. Whatever happened to *do unto others?* In places like this, decent people didn't leave each other stranded in the cold.

His face was feeling stiff, and he figured he'd better start walking before his toes went numb. He struck out for a distant yard light, the only sign of human habitation in sight. He couldn't tell how distant, but he knew he'd be hurting by the time he got there, and he was counting on some kindly old man to be answering the door. No shame among the lame.

It wasn't like Zach was fresh off the operating table—it had been a few months since his last round of repairs—but he hadn't given himself enough time. He'd lopped a couple of weeks off the near end of the doc's estimated recovery time, rigged up a brace, done some heavy-duty taping and climbed onto another bull. Hung in there for five seconds—four seconds past feeling the pop in his hip and three seconds short of the buzzer.

He could still feel the pain shooting down his leg with every step. Only this time he had to pick the damn thing up, swing it forward and drop it down again on his own.

Pride be damned, he just hoped *somebody* would be answering the door at the end of the road. The light in the front window was a good sign.

The four steps to the covered porch might as well have been four hundred, and he was looking to climb them with a lead weight chained to his left leg. His eyes were just as screwed up as his hip. Big black spots danced around with tiny red flashers, and he couldn't tell what was real and what wasn't. He stumbled over some shrubbery, steadied himself on the porch railing and peered between vertical slats.

There in the front window stood a spruce tree with a silver star affixed to the top. Zach was pretty sure the red sparks were all in his head, but the white lights twinkling by the hundreds throughout the huge tree, those were real. He wasn't too sure about the woman hanging the shiny balls. Most of her hair was caught up on her head and fastened in a curly clump, but the light captured by the escaped bits crowned her with a golden halo. Her face was a soft shadow, her body a willowy silhouette beneath a long white gown. If this was where the mind ran off to when cold started shutting down the rest of the body, then Zach's final worldly thought was, *This ain't such a bad way to go.*

If she would just turn to the window, he could die looking into the eyes of a Christmas angel.

* * * * *

*Could this woman from Zach's past
get the lonesome cowboy to come in
from the cold...for good?
Look for*
ONE COWBOY, ONE CHRISTMAS
*by Kathleen Eagle
Available December 2009 from
Silhouette Special Edition®*

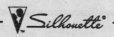

SPECIAL EDITION

We're spotlighting
a different series
every month throughout 2009
to celebrate our 60th anniversary.

This December, Silhouette Special Edition® brings you

NEW YORK TIMES BESTSELLING AUTHOR

KATHLEEN EAGLE

ONE COWBOY,
ONE CHRISTMAS

Available wherever books are sold.

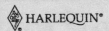

Silhouette®

SPECIAL EDITION

**FROM *NEW YORK TIMES* AND *USA TODAY*
BESTSELLING AUTHOR**

KATHLEEN EAGLE

ONE COWBOY,
One Christmas

When bull rider Zach Beaudry appeared
out of thin air on Ann Drexler's ranch,
she thought she was seeing a ghost of
Christmas past. And though Zach had
no memory of their night of passion years
ago, they were about to share a future
he would never forget.

*Available December 2009
wherever books are sold.*

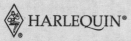

HARLEQUIN®

A Cowboy Christmas
MARIN THOMAS

2 stories in 1!

The holidays are a rough time for widower
Logan Taylor and single dad Fletcher McFadden—
neither hunky cowboy has been lucky in love.
But Christmas is the season of miracles! Logan
meets his match in "A Christmas Baby," while
Fletcher gets a second chance at love in "Marry
Me, Cowboy." This year both cowboys are on
Santa's Nice list!

*Available December
wherever books are sold.*

"LOVE, HOME & HAPPINESS"

www.eHarlequin.com

HAR75292

REQUEST YOUR FREE BOOKS!

2 FREE NOVELS
PLUS 2
FREE GIFTS!

◆ HARLEQUIN®

INTRIGUE®

Breathtaking Romantic Suspense

YES! Please send me 2 FREE Harlequin Intrigue® novels and my 2 FREE gifts (gifts are worth about $10). After receiving them, if I don't wish to receive any more books, I can return the shipping statement marked "cancel." If I don't cancel, I will receive 6 brand-new novels every month and be billed just $4.24 per book in the U.S. or $4.99 per book in Canada. That's a savings of close to 15% off the cover price! It's quite a bargain! Shipping and handling is just 50¢ per book.* I understand that accepting the 2 free books and gifts places me under no obligation to buy anything. I can always return a shipment and cancel at any time. Even if I never buy another book from Harlequin, the two free books and gifts are mine to keep forever.

182 HDN EYTR 382 HDN EYT3

Name	(PLEASE PRINT)	
Address		Apt. #
City	State/Prov.	Zip/Postal Code

Signature (if under 18, a parent or guardian must sign)

Mail to the **Harlequin Reader Service:**
IN U.S.A.: P.O. Box 1867, Buffalo, NY 14240-1867
IN CANADA: P.O. Box 609, Fort Erie, Ontario L2A 5X3

Not valid to current subscribers of Harlequin Intrigue books.

**Are you a current subscriber of Harlequin Intrigue books
and want to receive the larger-print edition?
Call 1-800-873-8635 today!**

* Terms and prices subject to change without notice. Prices do not include applicable taxes. Sales tax applicable in N.Y. Canadian residents will be charged applicable provincial taxes and GST. Offer not valid in Quebec. This offer is limited to one order per household. All orders subject to approval. Credit or debit balances in a customer's account(s) may be offset by any other outstanding balance owed by or to the customer. Please allow 4 to 6 weeks for delivery. Offer available while quantities last.

Your Privacy: Harlequin is committed to protecting your privacy. Our Privacy Policy is available online at www.eHarlequin.com or upon request from the Reader Service. From time to time we make our lists of customers available to reputable third parties who may have a product or service of interest to you. If you would prefer we not share your name and address, please check here. ☐

HIC

HARLEQUIN® HISTORICAL:
Where love is timeless

From chivalrous knights to roguish rakes, look for the variety Harlequin® Historical has to offer every month.

www.eHarlequin.com

HHBRANDINGBPA09

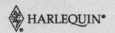
HARLEQUIN®

INTRIGUE

COMING NEXT MONTH

Available December 8, 2009

#1173 FIRST NIGHT by Debra Webb
Colby Agency
To prove his innocence, a talented artist caught up in a murder investigation is in a race against time to catch the true killer—with the help of a Colby agent. And if they can survive the first night, their growing attraction may have a chance as well.

#1174 HIS SECRET CHRISTMAS BABY by Rita Herron
Guardian Angel Investigations
He returns to his hometown determined to forget the past, but a missing child—and the child's adoptive mother—calls out the P.I.'s protective instincts. Can he save the family he never dreamed he'd have?

#1175 SCENE OF THE CRIME: BRIDGEWATER, TEXAS by Carla Cassidy
The small-town Texas sheriff has enough on his hands with a killer on the loose, but the feisty FBI profiler who insists on being a part of the case—against his wishes—may just be the woman he needs....

#1176 BEAUTY AND THE BADGE by Julie Miller
The Precinct: Brotherhood of the Badge
When the girl next door blows the whistle on illegal activities at work, the only person she can turn to for protection is her gruff cop neighbor—a man who is ready, willing and able to be her true-blue hero.

#1177 SECLUDED WITH THE COWBOY by Cassie Miles
Christmas at the Carlisles'
After rescuing his wife from a kidnapper, the cowboy is determined to seal the rift between them and remind her of their love. But when she comes under threat again, his actions may speak louder than words as he fights to save what's his.

#1178 POLICE PROTECTOR by Dani Sinclair
When she discovers that her sister and her sister's children are missing, a career-minded businesswoman turns to a take-charge detective to find them—and as he takes on the dangerous case, he shows her that family is what matters most....

HICNMBPA1109